HE WILL HAVE POWER OVER
ALL LIVING THINGS. . . .

The gates creaked open and the cage appeared, so large that it filled the opening. Reaching from above, someone released a latch. Then, with a scuffling and a creaking of wood, the creature bounded forth.

It was a sea-drake, far now from the salt spray on the western cliffs of its home. It bore no wings, being a swimming thing, but on its head rose a filigree crest. It was all lapped in silver scales; it stood twice house-high, yet pounced as lithely as a kitten. But Bevan rode out before it with eyes dazzled by its beauty.

All men gaped at him, that he could compel his horse to approach such a thing of terror. But as he drew near he slipped down from the steed and let it plunge away.

Bevan walked forward. The dragon bellied to the ground to meet him, sent forth a hoarse echoing cry and laid its great head on his shoulder. . . .

Books by Nancy Springer

The Sable Moon
The Silver Sun
The White Hart

Published by POCKET BOOKS

THE WHITE HART

Nancy Springer

PUBLISHED BY POCKET BOOKS NEW YORK

Another *Original* publication of POCKET BOOKS

**POCKET BOOKS, a Simon & Schuster division of
GULF & WESTERN CORPORATION
1230 Avenue of the Americas, New York, N.Y. 10020**

ISBN: 0-671-43131-5

First Pocket Books printing December, 1979

10 9 8 7 6 5 4

POCKET and colophon are trademarks of Simon & Schuster.

Printed in the U.S.A.

PROLOGUE

Long ago, so long ago that the enchantment of the Beginning was yet on it, there was a little land called Isle. It might have been the world entire for all the people knew; vast oceans encircled it even as the thick-woven Forest surrounded each village. Beyond the Forest, on the Wastes or the Wealds or the mountain Marches of the sea, the Old Ones yet walked; and gods, ghosts and all delvers in the hollow hills were no strangers to the woven shade just beyond the castle gates. It was in those times that *The Book of Suns* got its start, though the Sun Kings knew it only dimly; and a far-flung fate got its start when a lady fair as sunlight loved the Moon King at Laureroc.

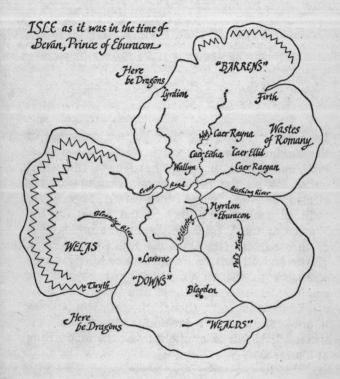

ISLE as it was in the time of
Bevan, Prince of Eburacon

"BARRENS"

Here
be Dragons

Lyrdion

Firth

Caer Rayna   Wastes
of Romany

Caer Eitha   Caer Ellid

Wallyn   Caer Raegan

Cross   Road   Rushing River

Myrilon

Gleaming River   •Eburacon

Killetty

WELAS   Pel's Nost

•Laveroc

"DOWNS"   Blagden
                        •
to Twyth

Here
be Dragons   "WEALDS"

BOOK ONE:

THE SPEAKING STONE

I sing the lady, the lightwinged maiden.

Golden as sunlight is Ellid Dacaerin;
Soft as dawn is the daughter of Eitha.

Bright as a sword is her soaring fancy;
Bold as a falcon her spirit flies.

Swift as the deer her sorrow leaves her;
Light as its leap her laughter rises.

Dauntless as fire is the dragon-daughter;
Fair as fire the light of her face.

Dearer than gold is the maid of Decaerin;
Warmer than gold is the glow of her eyes.

Longer than life is the troth of the lady;
Wider than worlds is the worth of her love.

CHAPTER ONE

It was a night of the dark of the moon, and darker yet within the narrow tower of Myrdon. Ellid shivered in her scant bed of short straw as much from dark as from cold. Never had she been so benighted. In her father's great hall the torches and tapers flared always to ward off the things that moved in the night: the wailing white ladies and the treacherous pouka who lured unwary travelers to death in pits or dismal fens. The black spaces of night swirled with such as these, and in the lofty chamber of her captivity Ellid sensed the swift denizens of air all about her. Naked as she was in the abyss of night, she shrank from their presence to no avail.

Yet when she heard noises of scraping and knocking close at hand, Ellid did not scream. Not for any peril would she have stooped to summon the rough men who laughed and feasted below. She only stiffened and hearkened intently. The sounds came from the high, barred window, now only a memory in the gloom. "Who is there?" Ellid whispered, and started violently when a soft answer came through the dark.

"A friend," the voice replied, a manly voice but sweet as singing. "Pray, lady, make no cry."

Hanging between hope and consternation, Ellid kept silence. She heard a grinding noise as the bars came loose and a thump as the stranger dropped to the floor. He moved toward her uncertainly, then stopped.

"Lady," he said in low tones, "it is black as Pel's Pit in here; I must make a light. Do not be afraid."

Ellid stared. "Mothers protect me!" she breathed. A pair of shining supple hands took form in the gloom, hands rimmed with ghostly light. Pale flames wavered at the fingertips. The hands cupped and lifted; Ellid glimpsed a face behind them, dark hollows of eyes and a chiseled jaw. The jaw tightened as the hands dropped.

"The vermin!" muttered the visitant. "That they must strip you!"

He came closer until he could touch the rough wall beside her; his hands left their light on the stone, like the specter of a star. By its faint glow Ellid could see the stranger but dimly. Still she deemed that he was slender and only little taller than herself. He knelt before her.

"This will not hurt," he said in his low, melodious voice, and she felt his fingers on her wrist. They were warm, as flesh of man is warm; she took some comfort in that. Inexplicably the fetters dropped from her arm. The stranger rose and stepped back from her. Ellid crouched against the stone like a creature at bay. Even naked as she was, she thought better of her own luck than of this eerie visitor in the night. He was no warrior in size; she could rush him, stun him against the stone perhaps, if he be in fact of human kind. . . . But even as she narrowed her eyes to spring, he pulled off his tunic and offered it silently to her.

She stood and put on the rough garment. It reached scarcely to her knees, but its warmth was like an embrace. The stranger brought a coil of rope and slipped a loop around her.

"I shall lower you slowly," he told her. "Feel your way with care—and unless all ill should chance, await me at the bottom. Are you ready?"

She knew now that she was obliged to trust him. She scrambled up and out the window without a word, hastening lest he should try to touch her and help her. Not even stumps of bars were in the window to hinder her. She clung to the sill as the rope tautened, then leaned against its slender strength as she felt her way downward. For the first time that night Ellid was thankful for the dark, not only that it hid her escape but that she might not see the dizzying drop below her. She strove not to think of it, nor of the weird hands that supported her, but of her enemies, the men of Myrdon. She went cannily, skirting windows, hugging the wall. When she felt cool earth under her bare feet at last, she tested it for long, incredulous moments before she loosened the rope from her shoulders at last.

Ellid gave a tug, and felt the answering tug from far above. She could not have said why she did not hasten away. Far better even to stumble alone through the night, many would have said, than to cleave to a warlock, one whose hands broke iron and shot fire. But it was not for cowardice that Ellid was called daughter to Pryce Dacaerin. She held the rope taut and awaited him to whom she owed some debt of thanks; she awaited one with warm hands and a soft voice.

Almost as quickly as her thoughts, he was beside her, skimming down the rope. To her renewed astonishment he pulled it down after him, so that it came tumbling about him. Quickly he coiled it and stowed it over his shoulder. Then, reaching surely even in the midnight darkness, he took her hand and started away. No speck of light showed on the walls; most likely the sentries had all joined the drunken feast that resounded from the great hall beyond the tower. The gates were barred, of course. Ellid's strange escort lifted the heavy beam and gently shoved open the timbered doors. Then he and the lady slipped through, and no cry followed them.

The first faint light of dawn found them leagues away, for the stranger walked quickly and surely even in the densest shadow of the trees. Ellid followed close behind, unable to see the sharp flints which cut into her bare feet, head lowered against branches which threatened to pierce an eye. The gray shade which presently filtered into the Forest showed her only the back of him who walked before her, naked above leather breeches and smooth as steel. But as they topped a ridge, quite suddenly they met the rising sun. It blazed full on their faces as the ground dropped away at their feet. Ellid lifted her arms thankfully, but her companion winced and turned away. "Come," he said. "All the world can see us here."

He plunged down the steep slope, and she followed, regarding him curiously. He was slender, and quite young, perhaps as young as she. His wideset eyes were as dark and glowing as coals. His hair was shining black, and his skin lustrous pale, like moonlight; his blood pulsed like a tide within. She had seen his lip come flashing red as he bit it. His face was faultless and strange, like a face in a dream. Ellid had never seen such stark beauty in a man; even in the daylight she looked askance at him.

In the shadows of the deep ravine they found a narrow stream. The youth knelt to fill his flask. Ellid sat and dabbled in the water with her smarting feet.

"Does the light hurt you?" she asked, breaking her long silence.

"I shall grow accustomed to it in time," the other replied gruffly. "Still, we must soon find shelter, my lady. Light is unlucky for the hunted."

Ellid inwardly steeled herself and struggled to her feet. But the search was not long. At the top of the next rise grew a grove of tall fir trees, with branches that swept heavily to the ground. Beyond was a sunlit space. The stranger lifted a thick green limb for Ellid to creep beneath.

"This is well," he said as he came in beside her. "We can see what comes to all sides. My lady, will you eat?" He offered her a small cake of oats and honey, such as the countryfolk placed on the ancient shrines. Ellid looked at it in surprise, but ate it gratefully.

"I owe you many thanks," she said as she finished, "for freeing me."

Her companion made a sound of genuine sorrow. "Ah, lady," he told her intensely, "I would have helped you days ago! I have followed since the day they stole you from your father's demesne. . . . Strong towers of stone make men careless, but on the road their guard was good. I could not get close."

The guard had indeed been good. Ellid's face

twisted wryly at the thought of the ten days' journey in the shameful cart, the jeers, the cuffs, the
floggings and the stinking food. The first day
they had cropped her hair to humiliate her. And
at journey's end they had stripped her even of her
humble shift. . . . Her face flamed to remember
it. The eyes that met hers were clouded with
misery.

"My lady, did they ravish you indeed?"

Ellid laughed harshly. "Nay! Nay, that at least
they did not. To men such as these, spoiled meat
is of no account, and I dare say they think my
worthiness to my father is the same. So they took
care to keep the wares whole, though they were
none too gentle in the transport."

"And I none too gentle in my rescue," the
dark-eyed stranger added bitterly. "To you who
deserve all good, I have offered a beggar's shirt
and a borrowed crust and the hard stones for
treading."

"Ellid Lightwing the bards have called me!
Could they but see me now!" Ellid smiled ruefully
at her painful, bloodied feet. "Yet my lot has
bettered a thousandfold. I owe you all thanks."
She spoke to him quite courteously. "What may
I name you, who have befriended me?" But he
turned away his raven-dark eyes.

"I answer to Sirrah," he muttered, "like other
sons of men."

Ellid frowned in puzzlement and said no more,
for she knew she would give him no slave's title.
The April sun was warm through the fir boughs,
and the thick bed of their dropped needles was
soft. Ellid stretched out her aching limbs. As she
dozed off to sleep she saw the black-haired youth

settle himself against the trunk of the tree, watching over her.

Hours later she awoke, alerted by some slight sound or sense of danger. She did not need her companion's hand on her arm to warn her to keep silence. On the hillside below rode the scouts of Myrdon, lazily probing the bushes with their spears. Tensely watching, Ellid could not doubt that they made their path toward the firs. To bide or to flee? Both seemed hopeless. But even as Ellid clenched herself in despair, the approaching men shouted and swerved from their course. In the valley beyond, a hart had broken cover. Ellid gaped; the deer was pure blazing white with a shine like a silver crown on its head. It was the loveliest creature she had ever seen. It posed like a carven thing for a moment before it flitted away, and all the riders of Myrdon galloped after it.

"So lightly are the sons of men turned from their intentions," the dark-eyed youth remarked dryly.

"Will you sleep now?" Ellid asked coldly. "I will watch." Her heart ached for the fleet white deer.

The stranger did not sleep, but sat silently beside her. Nothing more chanced that afternoon. In the twilight the fugitives crept forth, and discovered that they had sheltered in a sacred grove. The abode of the god was marked with a rough stone altar. Upon it sat some villager's offering of a few of last year's apples, now pecked by birds. The youth gathered them up and offered Ellid one. She creased her brow at him.

"Do you not fear the vengeance of the gods, that you pilfer their viands?"

"Nay, it is well enough," he answered vaguely. "Eat."

She took from his hand what she would not have taken from the shrine even had she been starving. But the food did little to ease her woes that night. Her feet were swollen and oozing, and the wood-soled sandals that her companion had lent her were clumsily large. They tormented her with stumbling and slipping until she returned them to their owner, preferring to brave the rocks. Her escort slowed the pace to ease her, but within a few hours her head swirled with feverish pain. She limped along dazedly, clinging to her companion's belt as much for support as for direction. She scarcely noticed when she fell and struggled to rise. Half-awares, she felt herself gathered up and slung over warm, smooth shoulders. She laid down her head and struggled no more.

Many leagues to the north, Cuin son of Clarric the Wise rode through the days beside his grim-faced uncle, Pryce Dacaerin; Pryce of the Strongholds, men named him. They went slowly, for they rode with an army at their backs, and matched their pace to the footpace of the kerns. Cuin chafed at the delay. He ached to speed as fast as horse could take him to the vile tower where Marc of Myrdon made his filthy nest. What might those ruffians be doing to Ellid!

"They will not dishonor her, if it is gold the rat of Myrdon would have from me," Pryce Dacaerin had told him. "Curb yourself, Sisterson."

And most likely it was gold. The whole land of Isle was rife with such extortions. Not within living memory, not since Byve had met his doom, had there been a High King to keep order. Clan holdings and chieftainships and petty kingdoms dotted the land, each within its own fortress and patch of fields; round them all the wildering Forest wrapped its labyrinth. Across it every summer the raiding parties wended like ships across sundering seas. . . . Perhaps it was not gold that Marc of Myrdon sought, Cuin reflected. Perhaps he would make Ellid a piece in some sneaking game of power, would flaunt her to tweak Dacaerin's nose. . . . Truly, having once seen her loveliness, could he fail to take her to his bed? Cuin clenched his fists at the thought.

He would gladly take his fair cousin to wife when they had regained her, even if she were dishonored. As he rode, Cuin envisioned her: a tawny sunlit thing, like a forest bird or a fleeting dappled deer. Her ways were free as the wind, headstrong indeed, but she never failed in the courtesy that comes from the heart. They had been good comrades for many years, and though she had not said him ay, still she had not said him nay. Indeed, the whole world expected that they would wed; it might be said that she was his birthright. Cuin's clan still cleaved to the old fashion of reckoning lineage through the woman. Thus he, the sister-son, was heir to his uncle's estate. But by his wedding Ellid, the uncle's child also might share; it was very just. And though Cuin was one who took direction ill, in this thing he was all obedience.

For Ellid born of Eitha had a face like a flower for loveliness and a body like a doe for grace; her mind was steadfast as a sword and her spirit was bright as its skylit blade. Cuin pressed on toward the tower of Myrdon with anguish in his heart, for he loved her well, as he would love her till he died.

CHAPTER TWO

Ellid awoke to find herself dappled in sunlight, lying beneath a ragged blanket on a thick bed of leaves. Not far away burned a campfire with an iron kettle hung above it. Overhead was a rude roof. . . . Ellid sat up to look around her, and gasped involuntarily as pain gripped her. The black-haired youth strode toward her from behind a wall of stone.

"What is it?" he asked.

"I ache, that is all." Ellid could see now that she was within a circular building, ruinous and half-open to the weather. Trees waved beyond; more she could not tell. Her rescuer brought her a tin cup of steaming liquid from his kettle. It was good meat broth spiced with herbs. Rabbit meat; she noted the skins stretched for drying nearby.

"The cure for your aches is close at hand," the youth said when she had finished "Lady, let me carry you once again." He lifted her up, blanket and all, and took her outside with graceful ease. Ellid's eyes widened. Before her rose towering spires of chiseled stone, ramparts and parapets and all the halls and chambers of a kingly court and keep: all silent, ravaged by fire and weather and half-hidden by living green. The chamber whence they had come was but a tiny gatehouse, dwarfed by the wall beyond. In some past age this had been a castle such as Ellid had never seen; nay, a city must have peopled these walls. Ten of her father's fortresses would not have made it up.

"What place is this?" she cried.

"Eburacon," the other replied. His soft voice vibrated with the word.

The lost home of the High Kings. Tales of that golden time were but fireside chatter to Ellid. She had paid them small mind, she who lived so ardently in her own era: What did it gain her that the land had not always been beset with petty war? But still the name rang through her like a half-remembered song. She hung silent with the wonder of it as the dark-eyed youth bore her rapidly through the vast and crumbling courtyard.

Presently they came to smooth stone steps descending to a walled grove of silver beech; great boulders of white stone tumbled among the trees. At the bottom of the dell they rounded a corner of stone and came upon a strange, bubbling pool of water in a smooth-worn basin of stone. Wisps of steam rose from the surface. Ellid's companion set her down on the brim and plunged in his fine-molded hands.

"There's marvelous power of strength and healing in this spring," he remarked, "and even were it foul the heat would bake the ache from you. Stay in as long as you like, my lady. There are no eyes to see you here, for this place is well guarded by the shades of the past. And when you are done, call me; I shall be about."

Ellid waited until his footsteps had faded well away before she took off her blanket and baggy tunic. The water was tingling-hot. She eased into it cautiously, but in a moment she had relaxed in delighted comfort. On a shelf below the surface she sat as securely as in a chair, and the water rippled up past her feet from some hidden vent below. Of all works of nature, Ellid had never known any so marvelous. She soaked in the warmth until beads of sweat formed on her face. Then she climbed out, slipped into her tunic and started gingerly back up the path.

She found her companion gathering deadwood in the courtyard. "My lady!" he exclaimed as he hastened toward her. "You should not be walking on those feet!"

"I do not know your name," she told him primly, "and could not summon you."

"Call me what you like!" he grumbled.

"Come, my lord." She faced him, smiling but quite serious. "What is it?"

For the space of ten breaths he probed her with his eyes that were deep and dark as wells. "My name is Bevan," he said at last. "Son of Byve High King in Eburacon. Born of Celonwy and fostered by her brethren under the hollow hills. Argent Hand, they called me."

"Then have I titled you too humbly in calling you lord," Ellid said in a small voice, "for you are one of the gods."

"Gods!" He laughed bitterly, but not, she sensed, at her. "Godlings. All are dwindled now, to the stature of mortals or less and to a span of some few hundreds of years. In the days of the glory of my father's kingdom, weeks of festival and sacrifice scarcely sufficed to do them honor. Now the miserable peasants scrape and starve to bring some small token to their altars. Greatly have washed the tides of time since the children of the mother goddess Duv gave up the sunlit lands to the Mothers of men."

He picked up Ellid then and strode with her back to their camp, he whose height was scarcely more than hers, and though he was slender he bore her lightly. He sat her down and fetched a basin of water for her feet, bathing them carefully and rubbing them with crushed herbs. Ellid watched the movements of his bare shoulders and his marvelous deft hands, and found no word to say to him.

"Nay," Bevan broke silence at last, "I am no more a god, my lady. I have cast in my lot with my father's folk. I who walk in the light must live quickly and die soon, as a man will."

"But why?" she gasped.

"Perhaps Duv knows. I do not know, except that my heart burned within me to go home to a people and place I had never known . . . to go home to die."

"Likely it will seem a short time to you," Ellid mumbled, somewhat discomfited by this talk of death, "but you must have many years left to you of a man's span. Though I dare say you are not as young as you seem."

"I scarcely know. Time moves differently in the torchlit castles of inner earth; indeed, it hardly seems to move at all." Bevan fronted her whimsically. "How long has it been in years of man since my father walked this way?"

"Some hundred years and more," she told him promptly. "Longer than the life of any man."

"Yet he was well in health when I left, though somewhat stooped. And I was born but lately in his age. Among my mother's people I am considered young, my lady."

"The High King Byve of Eburacon yet lives?" Ellid exclaimed. "Folk would have it that he died—"

"At the burning siege. Ay, dark are the powers of Pel Blagden, but that night he missed his prey." Bevan paused a moment, and his eyes took on a hard sheen. "That is another one who yet lives, my lady."

"Pel Blagden?" she whispered. "The mantled lord?"

"Ay. There are gods and there are gods, lady. Pel Blagden is one who did not set his finger to the Accord."

"Then no vow binds him, that he may not walk in the light. . . ."

"Ay, even so. He walks in many forms and bears many names. He feeds on strife and the blood of man, and he gathers treasure with dragon greed. He shames the memory of the great and gracious time—" Bevan shook himself. "Enough! It is sufficient evil that I have no bandaging for your feet." He smiled at her, the first smile she had seen on that pale, grave face, and well it became him. "Will you eat, my lady?"

They ate rabbit meat cooked with wild onions and wild carrot roots; Ellid could not wish for better. Then she had nothing to do but sit in the sun of the courtyard while Bevan scavenged amongst the ruins. He returned with iron spearheads and blackened swords, but no scrap of

cloth; all had rotted away years since. He took
a sword and chopped down a sapling, whispering
to it in some strange tongue before he touched
it. He made shift to fit it tightly to a spearhead,
lashing it on with his sandal-thongs. Then, wordlessly, he wandered off into the Forest which
spread all around. Ellid lay down where she was
and went to sleep.

She awoke to a feeling of strange, suspenseful
peace, so tangible that she could almost float in
it, like still water. The white hart stood watching
over her no more than ten paces away. Its eyes
were large, wideset and smoldering-dark, like
coals. The antlers on its head were silver and
curiously bent in the shape of a radiant crown.
Ellid looked and looked as if the sight would have
no ending, and the hart met her gaze. There were
apple trees growing in the courtyard, remnants
of what had once been a royal orchard in the
gardens of Eburacon. The stag turned regally and
slipped away between the fragrant boles; white
petals scattered over it. Ellid stirred and found
that Bevan was standing beside her.

"It is spring," he murmured, "and the apples
of Eburacon are in blossom."

"Folk say that the fruits are golden," Ellid said
absently, "and that it is death to eat them."

Bevan arched his brows. "No folk can come
here, but I wonder why they say that! Such apples
would seem the best of food to me."

The white hart stood beneath the snowy blos-
soms of the largest tree, and Ellid met its eyes
with love.

They stayed at ruined Eburacon for several
days. Ellid's feet healed quickly, and she went

about in slippers of rabbit skin to fetch firewood
and water for cooking. The place was running
with fountains of sweet water. They plashed into
deep pools where fat, lazy fish scarcely moved
from a human shadow; Bevan went in after them
with his bare swift hands. He gathered rabbits
from his snares, and on the second day he slew
a dappled deer; Ellid wore a kirtle of the skin.
They ate well, for there were plenty of greens
and tender sprouts for one who knew them. Bevan
gathered great delicious bunches. He brought
mushrooms, too, and Ellid had no fear of poison
in what he gave her.

"I pluck them by smell, mostly," he explained.
"Indeed, I often close my eyes to choose better.
You know I have small need of light. My mother's
people gather their food in moonlight and shadows—"

"And plait the horses' manes," she teased him,
"and ride the cows dry."

He smiled sourly. "All things that chance amiss
for man fall to the account of the children of
Duv! But in truth, many folk walk abroad in the
dim night that would wither in the light of day.
There is a frail and perilous beauty in the night."

Ellid knew that Bevan often roamed the dark.
He was feral as a cat, companionable through the
day but leaving with lean grace to prowl the night.
She did not wonder: Was not his mother the beau-
teous deity of the moon? Probably it was from
her that Bevan got his own fine-sculpted beauty,
his face of moonlight and shadow. Ellid watched
him often; she knew the lines of his chiseled
nostrils, the consummate shading of his temples
and grave mouth. His eyes were deep and wide
as night skies, and sometimes as aloof. When he

sat silent and withdrawn, it seemed to her that
he had left himself and gone to a place that was
closed to her, some secret realm. . . . She fancied
that he refreshed himself thus, and had no need
of sleep. His face brightened with the coming of
nightfall, and there was no sleep in his sparkling
eyes.

Once, waking from her own slumber, Ellid
heard him nearby, speaking in a tongue that
was strange to her; to whom or what she did not
know. "Do you often see your mother's people
in the night?" she asked him the next day as they
walked together.

"Never," he replied quietly. "I shall see my
mother and her folk no more, unless they should
choose to die as I have."

"Nor your father?" she asked, astonished.

"Nor he. I am quite apart now from that
world."

"Then you are very much alone," Ellid said
slowly. "Indeed why did you come, my lord? To
rescue fair maidens from towers?"

"Will you not call me Bevan?" he rebutted.

"When you call me Ellid," she smiled. "Come,
my lord: What brings you to the world of men?"

"By my troth, I know not!" Bevan looked not
at her, but far off into the trees as he spoke. "The
strange, strange world of men. The first day I
came, the rising sun smote me like swords. But
by noon I was better, and I traveled to a place
where men toiled, setting seed in the earth. I
watched them from the shadow of the trees, and
I wished nothing better than to toil with them,
touching the warm earth. I went to them at
last. . . ."

"What happened?" Ellid asked softly.

"They stared. Then a fat one came, and asked my business there, and seemed to take it ill that I had none. They took me to that same vile tower of Myrdon, my lady, and chained me by the kitchen door like a dog, stripped me and pelted me and offered me scraps to eat. When all was quiet, that night, I took off the chain and found some clothes and went away. Some soldiers traveled north the next day, and I followed them to see what they might be about, but I showed my face no more. Men are strange folk."

Ellid floundered for words. "Could you not— teach them better courtesy?"

"Nay." Bevan smiled ruefully at her. "Many things are amenable to my touch and my word, lady; stone and steel and fire will yield to me. But over men I have small power, unless they freely allow me. . . . Men are of all things most stubborn."

They walked a while in silence. "Yet men were not always so churlish," Ellid ventured at last.

"Ay, so I have heard." Bevan stopped his wandering feet and sat to face her. "When the Mothers ruled, like the Great Mother Duv who had granted the land to them, then was there peace for the most part, is it not so? For women are wont to nurture, not to destroy. I cannot understand why they ever gave the rule over to men."

"When men guessed that they, too, were makers of the children," Ellid said, "all fell to ruin. So my mother tells me, though that was long ago."

"Ay, what man would wish to leave his land to his sister's son over the child he himself has got?" Bevan stared before him, speaking as one who perceives with present sight. "Those were evil times! Cousin warred against cousin and brothers were wedded to sisters to share the heir. Even fathers turned against daughters. . . . And now the great wheel has turned indeed. Women's ancient arts of nurture are forgot; bards glorify only feats of war. The son names himself from the father, and his mother has become but a servant to him. Women are married away from their kinfolk, traded and thieved like so many cattle."

"Not in my father's house!" Ellid spoke up with pride. "We cleave to the old ways."

"Do you." Bevan came back to her with a wrenching effort. "Yet Pryce Dacaerin is a strong-fisted lord. Many are the soldiers he keeps in his hire."

"As he must. But you'll find no torturers in my father's house. Nor are the old courtesies forgot. No stranger goes away empty from my father's door, and honor is given where it is due, to the gods and to women. In all my father's business my mother's blessing goes with him."

"Then Pryce Dacaerin is a man to be honored as his wife." Bevan could not quite hide his amusement at her earnestness. "Where was he when you were taken?"

"Far away in Wallyn to the west," Ellid said stiffly, "as I am sure Marc knew well."

"I doubt it not." Bevan's dark eyes were sober now. "You love him well, your father."

"Ay." She could see him before her inward eye: a lean, craggy man, taller than other men; his hawk-red hair bristled like a living thing. Riding his blood-bay horse she saw him, but where? She reckoned the days. Five for the messenger to come to Wallyn bearing news like a slap in the face. A week or more for her father to return to his strongholds and muster his people. Even now he must be scarcely started on the ten days' journey to Myrdon. Ellid's heart yearned for him.

"You will be back to him within the week," Bevan told her, and meandered off into the Forest. Ellid sat and watched him go without comment; already she was accustomed to his unceremonious ways.

Bevan returned to their camp hours later, bearing some grouse for their supper. "The news has it," he remarked after he had helped her pluck the birds, "that your noble father set out from Caer Eitha three days ago, marching long and late. Already, it is said, he has come to the crossroads."

Ellid gaped at him, utterly taken aback. Bevan answered one of her questions before she could ask it. "Tree-spirits told me, for one," he explained quietly. "They do not travel, of course, but they hear all the chatter of the birds. And days ago I sent out shades—bodiless folk, they pass like the wind for speed. They bear out the report."

"My father must have ridden hard!" Ellid murmured.

"Could he think of you and do less?" For a moment Bevan's eyes on her were soft as twilight. Then he sighed. "I had hoped to wait until your feet were fully healed, and rightly shod, and until you were well in strength. But now we must go at once. There will be ill faring if Dacaerin should come to Myrdon without news of you."

"My feet will be well enough," Ellid stated, "as long as I can see the stones!"

"We must go by day then." Bevan looked at her with troubled eyes. "I dare say Marc of Myrdon still hunts for us, and there are ruffians about aplenty even if did he not! It will be no lark, my lady."

"Even so," she said.

"Even so. We will start tomorrow, early. Now come beside me here, and attend."

He drew a map in the dust of the floor. "Caer Eitha—the Wildering Way—Myrdon tower. We are here, to the east. We will go north and west, thus, to keep wide of Marc's haunts and yet hope to meet your father. If you keep a line between the setting sun and the constant star, you will cross the road sometime. . . ."

"But my lord," Ellid whispered, "will you not be with me?"

"I will if we are not beset." He faced her candidly. "But if it comes to fighting, my lady, you must flee with all haste and go on alone. Do not look to me for deliverance from force of arms, for I have no fighting skill. You must look only to save yourself. Promise me."

She faced him numbly.

"Ellid!" he urged.

"I promise," she mumbled.

"That is well. Now must you eat well, and sleep well. The morning will be soon in coming."

Ellid ate her meal in anxious silence. She had hardly realized how her contentment had grown in Eburacon. Eager as she was to rejoin her father, yet she found herself sorry to leave this peaceful place. Outside of the invisible wall which surrounded this protected spot was a world of

senseless strife. Ellid had lived in that world all
her life with hardly a shiver; yet now the thought
of it filled her with dread. Shapes of terror
crowded in on her as they had crowded that night
in the tower, but this time they were shapes of
human evil. Ellid would not say it even to herself:
the blackest terror was the fear of losing Bevan.

As the shadows deepened she bathed one last
time in the warm spring. But it could not heal the
anguish of her mind. When night fell she went to
her couch of leaves and lay tensely staring into
the gloom. Sleep was long in coming, and when
it came at last she got no good of it; dreams
racked her. It seemed that she was once again
in the hands of Marc's men, but this time she
was not able to put the bold face to it as she had
before. She cried out when they slapped her, and
they laughed. They stripped her and she huddled
before them, whimpering, hating herself; then she
realized that they meant to ravish her. She
screamed and struck out wildly, writhing to free
herself from the hard hands which pulled her
about. It was no use; someone had her by the
shoulders. . . .

"Ellid! Ellid! It is I, Bevan!"

Seeing his pale face by the faint light of em-
bers, she could not realize at first where she was.
Then she who had not winced for all of Marc's
ill usage hung her head and wept helplessly.
Bevan gathered her into his arms.

". . . don't know what I am crying for," Ellid
choked.

"For sorrow: Is it not enough?" Bevan settled
himself against the wall and cradled her against
his chest. "Sorrow will turn to stone unless you

weep. I thought it would come before this. Weep
it out."

She cried into the collar of his rough peasant
shirt, feeling him warm and lean beneath the
cloth. How strange that one so slight could be so
strong, to carry her weight for her when she could
not. How far had he carried her . . . ? When she
tired of weeping, she lay quietly with her hand
on his neck. She lay while happiness crept like a
tiny animal into the darkened hut. She scarcely
breathed, so as not to frighten it.

"Ellid?" Bevan whispered, and then he slowly
and carefully laid her down, thinking she was
asleep. She felt him kiss her face; his lips were
light as moth's wings on her lidded eyes. Then
he went away, and in a moment, so it seemed, it
was morning.

To start their journey they had but to eat and
walk away, so few were their possessions. Bevan
tied a rusty sword at his waist. Ellid carried her
ragged blanket, a spoon and a tin cup. Bevan took
his spear for a staff, and without a word they set
out. They strode along carelessly until they came
to the long barrows where lay the shattered bones
of the guardian shades. Then they glanced at
each other, set their teeth, and more cautiously
went over. Eburacon was behind them now.

CHAPTER THREE

They had not journeyed more than half a day when that which Bevan dreaded came to pass.

It was surely one of the oddest battles ever waged. As Bevan and Ellid traversed a wooded valley, two men on horseback came plunging down the scarp. "Flee, Ellid!" Bevan cried, and loosed his spear; it flew wide. He ran straight at the speeding riders, shouting crazily, tugging at the clumsy sword which tangled in his belt. War-trained though they were, the horses shied from him, and one slipped on the steep turf, throwing its rider heavily to the ground. The other man, fighting for balance and waving his sword overhead, fairly skewered himself on Bevan's outstretched blade. The horses, relieved of their burdens, shook themselves and wandered away; Bevan stood staring at the prostrate forms before him, and Ellid came up beside him to stare in turn.

"I thought I bade you flee," he told her without heat.

"There was no time!" she answered dazedly. "What ails that one?"

Bevan went to check him then. "I think his neck is broken," he reported. "Ellid, catch the horses, and keep away from here."

The horses were foraging at no great distance. Ellid went to them gently and caught them easily by their trailing reins. Bevan was stripping the bodies. Only a cloth badge marked them as men of Myrdon; he tore it off. Otherwise they wore the motley common to men of the day. One tunic was spoiled with blood. He bundled it into the bushes with the bodies and went to Ellid with his booty.

"Here," he said gruffly. "Put on this gear to cover yourself."

She went aside and dressed in a tunic, knee breeches and sandals. The clothes were overlarge and still sickeningly warm from their previous owner, but she grimaced and put them on as best she could. When she returned she found Bevan also changed and rummaging a shirt for himself from the horses' baggage. "You make a pretty lad," he greeted her. "Do you think you can ride?"

Ellid regarded the horses in dismay. These were battle beasts, as sour and quarrelsome as their former masters, and harnessed only with halters and blankets, for saddles and bits were not things then thought of. Moreover, she had never sat on any horse, not even the tamest. "You must know it is not fit for a woman to straddle a horse!" she told Bevan. "It will harm the—virgin zone."

He snorted. "That is a saying of men."

She gaped at him. "You mean—the Mothers rode, in those other times?"

"The Mothers, and my mother, though not lately. There is small keeping of steeds under the hollow hills. Indeed, I have never ridden, but I must attempt it; I lack a virgin zone." He regarded her in sober mockery.

Ellid did not like being put on her mettle. She glared at him and chose her horse forthwith, scrambling onto it from a stump. Bevan vaulted onto his and led off on their interrupted journey. They went silently, ducking branches, concentrating on their new mode of travel. When the horses grew unruly, Bevan spoke to them in his strange tongue and corrected them as if they were thoughtless children. At dusk they tethered the animals and made camp. Ellid kept icy silence, and Bevan was grave as usual. There were blankets and bread in the horses' packs; Ellid was grateful to be fed and warmed. But once again, though she lay in the snuggest bed she had known for many days, Ellid could not find sleep.

She arose at last and looked around with night-sharpened eyes. On the brow of a nearby hill she could see Bevan sitting in the dim light of a quarter-moon. Ellid thought she had never seen a lonelier figure. A fortnight before she would not have ventured out after dark with a sconce of candles in her hand, but this night she started up the rough, wooded hill without a second thought.

As she approached she could hear Bevan softly singing:

"Death is a grisly King;
　　Fate is his bride.
　Now quaintly I've chosen
　　To serve at their table,
　　To dance at their wedding. . . ."

Bevan broke off his song as Ellid neared the top. He reached out to her and made room on his rock.

"The blood of that Marc's man still splatters on my mind," he said after a while. "Is that what ails you also, daughter of Eitha?"

She shook her head.

"Then what sends you roaming the night, Ellid?"

"Chance Duv knows!" She spoke lightly. "Folk have always told me that the night is full of all manner of evil."

"Ay, even so," Bevan said heavily, "but it is the same evil that is in the day—evil of men. Look there!"

On hilltops all around sparks of light were springing up, wherever cleared land lay. It was the eve of the first of May, the festival of the Consort god Bel, and throughout the land folk were kindling need-fire against plague and famine. . . . Ellid laughed aloud. On this night of all others, folk said, the demons of the Otherworld sped on their fell errands, and only fiercest fire could keep them off. Yet here she sat beside a white-handed warlock under the dim light of a crescent moon, and she felt as safe as she had ever been in her father's great hall.

Bevan smiled at her merriment, but there was no mirth in his eyes. "Why do you laugh?" he asked in honest puzzlement.

"For folly." Ellid sobered. "I should not have laughed, Bevan, while you are sore of heart."

"Nay, it is better to laugh. I should laugh, too, thinking of myself, what fool I am! I have left the fair halls of the moonlit folk to join a people who hide behind fires. . . . What folly is mine! How can I ever hope to befriend these suspicious folk, strange thing that I am? I am like a leper that hangs in his hut between earth and sky, part of neither. I am kin to no one, and no one touches me. . . ."

Ellid touched his fair hand where it lay clenched upon the stone. He startled like a deer.

"Except for one, the very daughter of the Mothers," he said softly. "Ellid Ciasifhon we would call you in my tongue, Ellid Lightwing. But you have been angry with me this day, my lady."

"The more folly mine." She took the tightened hand, smoothing it between her own. "Be of better cheer, Bevan."

He trembled at her caress, turned to her lips with trembling lips. His kiss went through her like fire; she had never known feeling to match it. They filled each other's arms. They thought their passion filled the night. "Can mortal kisses always be so sweet?" Bevan breathed in wonder at last.

"I believe that was among the best," Ellid faltered.

"Were that all of comfort that this world of men had to offer me, still it would be enough."

Ellid went late to her bed that night and slept smiling. The next day she and Bevan rode quietly, for sometimes eyes were upon them. They traversed villages and hard-cleared plots amidst the vast random Forest. They ate the honeycakes they found set before the village shrines and watered their horses at the sacred wells; folk shrank from before them and let them pass. When the dark came they sat in silence, letting their lips speak without words, and presently Bevan left to roam the night as was his custom. In the morning they kissed and rode on. But they did not ride until dark that day, for in mid-afternoon they found the Wildering Way.

They camped in thick Forest atop a hill near the track. Ellid kept watch over the Way while Bevan went to forage. He returned at dusk with rabbits and news. "Word is that your father is less than a day's march to the north," he told her. "We may as well await him here."

They cooked and ate wordlessly. "Share my bed this night," Ellid said to him when they were done.

"My loins long for you," Bevan answered simply. "But still I would send you back to your father a maid."

She lifted her head proudly. "In times past, women of my line have lain with whom they would, and answered to no one."

"I know it," he said, "but then is not now. And I who am a filcher of shrines am not likely to become your husband, though it will not be for want of wishing. . . . Have you no sweetheart, Ellid?"

"Cuin who is my cousin and my father's heir," she replied slowly, "would wed me gladly. But we are not betrothed; always I have put him off with excuses. . . . He is a brave heart, and loyal, and we have long been the best of friends. Indeed I could scarcely explain even to myself why I would not give him my promise. But now I think I know why."

"You will wed him in the end," murmured Bevan, half to himself.

"Perhaps." She faced him steadily. "His people and mine expect it. Yet I have never felt for him what I feel for you, Bevan son of Byve. And as

I live and am woman, my body must answer to my heart."

"I will not lie with you," Bevan told her heavily. "I would be a coward to sow where I cannot expect to stay. . . . Ellid, you know I am yours, in soul if not in all. Can you not be content?"

She regarded him where he sat grave and pale in the silver moonlight. "Argent Hand, they called you," she murmured. "I think your soul is in your hands of power as much as in the rest of you. Bevan, come to me and touch me, and I shall know that we have loved."

He arose and came with her to her bed under the shadows of the trees. He lay beside her in the dark and caressed her with his hands that could melt steel; his touch was as warm and tingling as the healing spring of Eburacon. He lay beside her as she slept under his hand, and he lay there yet when she awoke in the gray dawn, though she knew sleep was a stranger to him. He kissed her in that pale light, then arose and went from her, and she closed her eyes tightly against the coming of that day.

"There they are," Bevan said.

Ellid could plainly see in the distance the glint of many spears, bright in the midday sun. The red dragon, her father's device, waved over them. Bevan sighed and rose to get his horse. Numbly Ellid started to fetch hers, but Bevan stopped her with a touch on her arm.

"Ride before me this one time," he said, "for the sake of your virgin zone." He smiled crookedly, but Ellid could not answer his smile; she did not have the jester's gift of mocking pain.

Bevan set her sideways on his horse and got

up behind her, cradling her close against his chest.
They waited in silence as the dark mass of men
and steeds drew nearer.

"There is my father at their head," Ellid said,
"on the red bay."

Bevan nodded. "Who is on the roan by his
side?"

"Cuin."

They bided their time until the vanguard entered the defile just below their camp. Ellid had
laid her head on his shoulder. Bevan kissed her
tenderly.

"If I live, Ellid born of Eitha," he promised her,
"I will come to you."

She clung to him one more moment, then raised
her head. Bevan sent the steed forward at the
canter. He raised his right hand high in token
of friendship as they broke cover. The army shuddered to a halt as its leaders turned to face the
strangers. Pryce Dacaerin set his hand to his
sword hilt. Beside him, brown-haired Cuin was
as tense as himself.

"My father!" Ellid called.

Pryce Dacaerin's jaw sagged in amazed relief.
He had scarcely time to whisper "Daughter!" before the dark-eyed stranger had come up beside
him and set her in his arms. Pryce embraced her
hard, then took her by the shoulders and gazed
on her. She was crop-haired and somewhat thin,
but plainly whole.

"Father," she said, "here is one who has befriended me. Pray speak him fair."

It was a raven-haired youth, no warrior in
build, but there was something of power in the
quiet way he sat his big horse. "What boon I

have to grant is yours for the asking," Pryce said recklessly.

"I ask no boon, lord," the other replied, "except that you hear me. It is a rare man who will abide to be schooled by a youth and a stranger."

"Say on," Dacaerin told him.

"Go warily, my lord. There is some mischief afoot in Myrdon. When I went to find my lady, I saw a large structure of wood somewhat removed from the great hall, with strong guard all around. I thought perhaps they had put their captive there until I heard the talk of the sentries. They spoke of the lady in the tower and of that which they guarded; Dacaerin's bane, they called it, and laughed at the welcome it would give you. I do not know what it could be."

"Some new engine, I dare say," Pryce replied. "I thought it strange that Marc should beard me thus, but this explains it. He has got his hands on a toy and must have his play. . . . Will you not take some boon from me, you to whom I owe many thanks?"

"Someday, perhaps. Not this day."

"Stay and eat with us, at least," Pryce urged with the politeness that expects to be refused.

"Nay, I must go. My lord, my lady, all good come to you."

He saluted and wheeled quickly away, but Ellid called after him, a call clear as a plea: "Bevan!"

He pivoted his horse to face her. "My lady?"

What was she to tell him, in front of all present? "Many thanks," she said at last, and watched him ride away until the woven shade of the Forest took him. Her people crowded around her, but she scarcely heard them.

"By himself that one freed you from the tower of Myrdon?" Cuin demanded.

"Ay," she said.

"Daughter, are you still a maid?" Pryce Dacaerin asked her.

"Ay," she said again, and wondered vaguely at the question.

"Cuin," Dacaerin told his nephew, "pick a dozen good men to go with you, and guard her carefully home."

Cuin stared in silent protest. "Ay," Pryce said roughly, "I know you long to thrust your sword at Marc's doom. But there is no one whom I trust so well to see her back to her mother's side, and you are not yet her man, that vengeance should be yours. Go now."

Cuin bit his lip and went to choose his troop. Within the hour Pryce Dacaerin was on the march again toward Myrdon, and Ellid was riding north on a pillion behind Cuin son of Clarric. She went silently, and her eyes looked far away, for in the fringes of the Forest she had seen a white hart stand.

CHAPTER FOUR

Three days later Pryce Dacaerin came to the walled tower of Myrdon and ranged his army around. Then with the strange, scornful courtesy of war, he rode alone to the ponderous gates and roared for Marc to parley. Marc shouted an insulting reply from the platform of his tower. The petty lord of Myrdon tried to bluff that he still held Ellid captive, but he soon found that Pryce knew better. Dacaerin demanded a huge sum of gold as a face-price. Failing that, as he knew he would, he challenged Marc to single combat. Marc rebutted with accusations of plotted treachery and bade Dacaerin take him as best he could. After a final shouted exchange of threats and indignities, Pryce rode back to his waiting army. It was almost dark. On the morrow battle would be joined.

Dacaerin set stiff guard that night, and did not fear that the senrties would doze at their posts, for the whole camp was restless with anticipation. Pryce himself felt small desire for sleep and sat late in his tent instructing his captains. He sent them to their beds at last and stood at his tent flap studying the night. Without a light or the sound of a footfall, a shadow moved before him and a voice said, "My lord?"

Pryce sprang back and drew his sword. "Who goes? Let me see you!"

He gaped at the slim, black-haired youth who stepped into the firelight. "You! You have startled me; I am not accustomed to be so crept up on. How did you come here?"

"Pardon, my lord." Bevan's face was grave and anxious. "For courtesy I should have come to the guards, but in truth I never thought of it. I am like a cat, my lord; in the night I go where I will."

"Even as you went to my daughter's prison cell."

"Even so."

"Come and sit by the fire. What do you want with me?"

Bevan sat, but kept somewhat back from the flames. "For some few nights now, my lord, I have prowled about this fortress of Myrdon. The guard is good, but tonight at last I got onto the roof of that great wooden house of theirs. It is some large living thing that they keep captive there. I heard it breathe. I could not see it or speak to it, to tell you more."

Pryce Dacaerin's ruddy face went bleak with this news. Though he had never seen any of the huge and ancient creatures that men call enemy, he knew that such still roamed in the vast wilds of Isle, especially in the steep lands to north and west. "Did it breathe hot?" he demanded.

"Nay, my lord. It could scarcely be a fire-drake, not in a cage of wood. A griffin, perhaps, or a wyvern; some cold thing of earth or flood."

"How ever could that coward Marc have got such a prize?" Pryce muttered.

"Some trickery." Bevan leaned forward earnest-ly. "My lord, I would beg a boon now."

"Speak."

"When they loose it on you, whatever it may be, bid your men stand back and hold their weap-ons. Let me face it."

Pryce gazed on him in pity and surprise. "You are not one who is thewed for war," he said.

"Nay, my lord, I have no skill of arms, for I would be a friend to all who crave friendship. Let me speak to it, I mean. I hope I can turn its wrath."

Dacaerin shook his head wearily at this folly. But he had promised the boon and must needs assent. "What was it my daughter called you?" he asked at last.

"Bevan."

"One nobly born who has no inheritance," Pryce Dacaerin mused on the name. "What is it that you seek, Bevan? Glory? A taste of fortune, perhaps?"

"Not glory, surely. Though I will not deny that I also have some quarrel with Marc of Myrdon." Bevan's eyes glowed darkly, like black coals that have flickered for a moment into flame. Then he smiled faintly at some private jest. This lord would never understand his true reasons, he knew. . . . "Shall we but say that I seek the favor of the gods?" he proposed.

"Then the gods defend you on the morrow," Da-caerin replied dryly, and he smiled sourly as he watched the visitor go. He had seen a long look pass between this one and his daughter, and he judged that either her person or her dowry was on Bevan's mind. Little he guessed that the dark-eyed youth thought most this night of the lonely

form of some great creature of earth, imprisoned
in the dark beyond Myrdon's walls.

Early the next morning Pryce Dacaerin set to
hurling his kerns against the hard walls of Myrdon. Soon he noted Bevan sitting quietly on his
horse at the Forest's edge. It irked Dacaerin that
the youth did not offer to fight, but at present
there was no work for horsemen, only tight work
on scaling-ladders. Pryce shrugged and turned his
back on the silent watcher.

It was mid-morning, and many wounded lay
beneath the walls, when Dacaerin's captains
brought word that the men of Myrdon were wheel-
ing a huge wooden cage to the gates. Pryce was
not loath to fall back as he had promised. If
Marc's men then poured out of the gates, so much
the better; he could bring his riders to bear on
them. He withdrew his troops to the Forest line
and waited.

Presently the clumsy gates creaked open and
the cage appeared, so large that it filled the opening. Reaching from above, someone released a
latch. The cage was shoved through the gate as
Myrdon's men cautiously peered from behind it.
Then, with a scuffling and a creaking of wood,
the creature bounded forth.

"Child of the very deep!" Bevan breathed.

It was a sea-drake, far now from the salt spray
on the western cliffs of its home. It had no wings,
being a swimming thing, but on its slender head
rose a filigree crest. It was all lapped in silver
scales which shone blindingly bright in the sunlight; it stood twice house-high, yet pounced as
lithely as a kitten. Pryce Dacaerin thought that he
had never seen anything so fearsome. He felt his

armies shrink at the sight of it. Beyond it the men of Myrdon cheered and followed in its path. But Bevan rode out before it with eyes dazzled by its beauty.

All men gaped at him, that he could compel his horse to approach such a thing of terror. But as he drew near he slipped down from the steed and let it plunge away. The silver dragon crouched at him, hissing, glaring with flat amethyst eyes. He spoke to it, and then took the rusty sword from his belt and sent it spinning far away over the battle plain.

"Lunacy!" Dacaerin muttered.

"*O irmelbeteyn, kish elys a that ondde?*" Bevan was speaking in the elder tongue of earth. ["Oh my lovely one, what have they done to you?"] The dragon lashed its shining tail as it trembled out its story of rage. The cold, pounding wrath of stormy seawater was in its voiceless communication, and the dark purple danger of the stiller depths, the outrage of an ancient surging elemental force now prostituted by men. But above all, from those pebble-hard violet eyes, Bevan learned of the motherhood of the Old Ones who walked before the Mothers or the mother goddess Duv. For the dragon was daughter of those whose females were smiting strong and never tamed, and she had proudly borne her own get: proudly, until the men of Myrdon came and took it from her.

"*O, irmelbeteyn,*" Bevan whispered, and his dark eyes filled with pity like balm of the quiet goddess of night. "Oh sweet, wild child of the sea . . ." Bevan walked forward, and the dragon bellied to the ground to meet him, sent forth a

hoarse echoing cry and laid its great head on his
shoulder.

The silence after the cry was like a blow. Men
of both armies stood thunderstruck as Bevan
stroked the gleaming scales. "They who have hurt
you are sheltering in your wake," Bevan murmured, and had no need to say more. The dragon
raised its head. Bevan swung to a perch on its
smooth shoulders, clinging below the crest of its
curving neck. The sea-drake rose to its fullest
height, wheeled with deadly grace and charged
full upon the forces of Myrdon. Pryce Dacaerin
stared for only a moment before he shook himself
and his troops into action.

The sea-drake attacked and slew with desperate
power. All about its feet flowed blood of men and
beasts. On his lofty seat Bevan was safe from
blows but as helpless as one who rides a wave,
helpless to aid his mount's reckless revenge. The
dragon ran like a tide, breaking herself upon her
enemies. Not even at the siege of Eburacon,
where Byve High King broke his sword and lost
his crown, must such despairing fervor have been
seen. Byve had not touched a weapon since that
evil night. . . . Bevan winced and shut his dark
eyes to the carnage all around him. Strange was
the fate that had sent Byve's son to another such
scene of bloody rout.

For the defeat of Marc's soldiers was swift and
complete. Picking his way through the mangled
results, Pryce Dacaerin found the raven-haired
youth sitting with the dragon's silver head in his
lap. "Put by your sword if you come here," Bevan
said unceremoniously as the lord drew near. "The
steel hurts her."

Without comment Dacaerin gave his weapon to a servant, then squatted by Bevan to study the powerful beast that now lay like a huge lump on the ground. The once-smooth silver body was battered and torn, but Pryce could see no deadly wound.

"Her heart is gone," Bevan said softly in reply to his unspoken query. "They stole her little one while she hunted in the sea—a tiny thing, scarce bigger than a cow. They lured her hither with it, wore away her strength with the weary miles, and once they had caged her they slew it before her eyes. They tormented her with steel, also; even the sight of iron or steel is agony to the Old Ones. When they loosed her at last, she was ready to avenge herself on anything that bore the name of man."

"Except you," Dacaerin remarked.

Bevan made no reply, only caressing the crested head which was delicately wrought for all its bulk. In a moment the dragon breathed its last and the silver sheen flickered out of its eyes.

"The rat of Myrdon has taken refuge in his stony nest," Dacaerin broke silence. "Would you come with me to find him?"

Bevan wondered wryly at this unwelcome token of Dacaerin's regard. Perhaps the older man sensed how little he cared for the ways of war. He would have liked to thwart Pryce's ill-intended courtesy, but the man was Ellid's father. And truly there was some cause to wish Marc dead. . . .

"Let this dragon not be touched," Bevan said.

Dacaerin posted guard over the sea-drake's body. Then, with retainers at their backs, he and Bevan entered Myrdon tower. In the great hall,

men and women huddled disconsolately under
guard, awaiting a life of servitude. Pryce Dacaerin
strode past them with hardly a glance and took
to the stairs. In the upper chambers some few
men still lurked.

Most of them yielded easily. Marc of Myrdon
stood at bay by his treasure-room door, and he
did not yield, for he knew that he might not expect even the dubious mercy of slavery. Dacaerin
addressed his sword, for his was the blood-right,
and blood in plenty met his need. He sent Marc's
sword flying with his third stroke, and after that
he took his time with his revenge, dealing slashing
blows that would not quite kill or even stun. Marc
was a screaming lump on the tower floor before
he grew quiet at last. Bevan watched with a face
gone hard and tight. He had forgotten to hate
Marc.

"Come!" said Pryce when he was finally done.
"Let us see to the spoils!"

He booted Marc's body to one side. It took
several men to pry off the mighty bolts on the
treasure-room door. Then Pryce and his followers
all poured into the dim chamber, jubilant at the
sight of the fine-wrought gold piled about the
walls. "Would you look at that!" one man exclaimed.

In the center of the room stood a tall shape like
a chalice, gleaming reddish-gold and rimmed with
pearls; altar-high it was, and of a great weight.
Set into the top was a stone larger than a man's
head, earth-colored, round and smooth. Bevan
stood darkly at the door, but when his gaze fixed
on this he walked to it and placed his hands upon
it, priestlike. A voice deep as the depths of time

sounded through the room: "Hail to thee, High King of Isle! Hail to thee, heir of Byve and of Veril and the mighty sons of the Mothers!"

Men jumped and stared, but Bevan stood still as the stone.

"Cherish the white hart, son of Byve," it intoned in accents eerie with antiquity. "Let thine eyes never behold the sea, lest the blood of the Otherworld flow to full tide in thee. May thine heirs ever stand the stay of Isle against the evil from the east. The blessing of the Great Mother be on thee. Thrice Hail to thee, High King of Isle!"

Like one released from a trance, Bevan dropped his hands and stepped back from the stone.

"Keep this to yourselves," Dacaerin told his men sternly and sent them out of the room. He shut the heavy door behind them and turned to Bevan. "What is the meaning of this?" he demanded.

"This must be the Stone of Destiny," Bevan murmured, "that stood of old amidst the fair fountains of Eburacon. . . ."

"That cries out in a human voice to proclaim the coming of a Very King," Pryce finished impatiently. "This I know. But what are you?"

Bevan sighed and faced him. "Byve High King did not die at the sack of Eburacon," he replied. "I am his heir. But little I thought to claim it. Strange is the fate that brought the Speaking Stone under my hands."

"Not so strange, indeed. The rats of Myrdon were lackeys of the mantled lord in that time; likely he threw them this bauble as a sop." Dacaerin spoke absently, as if struggling with many thoughts. "But you need not have touched it this day, my lord."

Bevan regarded him dryly. "I am no lord at present," he retorted, "nor entirely a fool. But I believe I could not have kept away from it. I was as one drawn."

"Even so." Pryce collected himself. "What may be your plans, Bevan of Eburacon?"

"Plans?" Bevan nearly smiled. "I am a creature of the wilds, my lord. Does the deer plan its seasons?" He turned to the massive door and opened it with a touch. Dacaerin jumped to follow him out.

"When you have need, Bevan, let me aid you," he said eagerly.

Bevan scarcely nodded. Pryce Dacaerin strode toward the door, but as he passed the Speaking Stone, he hesitated. Cautiously he laid a hand on it, then snatched it back as stinging pain shot through him. He cursed under his breath, and furtively glanced toward the doorway to see if Bevan had noticed. But the raven-haired youth had vanished.

It was scarcely to be expected of human frailty that Dacaerin's men should keep secret the wonder of the Stone. Within minutes after they left the treasure room, the tower of Myrdon buzzed with excited talk.

The most loyal of Dacaerin's men said that it was he who would be the High King, for who could think it of a slender-thewed youth with no skill in arms? He had been but the means of the Stone's speech, a priest or seer. These men insisted that the Stone had said "heir" to Byve High King only meaning a successor. Pryce Dacaerin

was the man so destined: had he not stood by
even as the Stone prophesied?

Others thought of Bevan's weaponless power
that had turned the dragon, and these declared
that he must be a true heir of the very blood of
Byve. One man who had been in the treasure
room even swore that the Stone had said "son of
Byve." He was heartily laughed down, for had not
Byve been dead these hundred years and more?
If ever he had a son it was a brat, for he had
never been wed to men's knowledge. But even a
brat of Byve would have been a power to be
looked to. Talk swirled for many days around the
slight remembered form of Bevan.

Pryce Dacaerin had thoughts like these and
many more. If his daughter were to marry the
youth, would it make her a Queen and himself a
King's advisor? Or should he try to appropriate
the Stone's words to himself and build himself a
throne of them? Pryce Dacaerin had accumulated
his own sizable holdings by seizing a chance
where it offered, and he had undone many a
worthy opponent. Moreover, he somewhat disliked
the slender, dark-haired youth. He had sensed
Bevan's aloofness, his distaste and his graceful
evasions. But he had also sensed the Prince's ar-
cane powers, so different from his own, and he
was wary of challenging him openly. Still, he
failed to think what other power threatened him
and all of Isle.

For the news of the Speaking Stone traveled,
as news will, in ways mysteriously rapid, until it
came to the attention of the cloaked god who
dwells in the darkest of valleys, of the mantled
lord who was ancient when Pryce Dacaerin was

a babe. And this mantled one rose up in anger and agitation: for he knew quite well that the Stone of Destiny did not speak for so meager a man as Pryce Dacaerin.

CHAPTER FIVE

Caer Eitha was nothing more than a boxlike walled fortress of stone, set in a clearing lonely as an island amidst the encircling sea of Forest. Pryce Dacaerin had named the unlovely stronghold after his wife, as a man will who rates his women with his possessions. He ruled other such strongholds which he called after his daughter and his sister, his mother and her kin. The device of the red dragon flew over them all. Without doubt Pryce Dacaerin was the most powerful man in Isle of that day. Marc of Myrdon was a mad fool to challenge him. But yet his reach had come to the limits of its grasp, and still no man called him King.

It was to Caer Eitha that Cuin son of Clarric took his cousin Ellid. By the time he brought her home a scowl had settled on his handsome face, for Ellid had been like a stranger: quiet, solitary and aloof. She had not kissed him even for greeting. Her mother also noted the change in her, and said that she was fatigued from her ordeal. Cuin wished that he could think the same, but suspicion nagged him; the more so because he scorned to give it voice. Only in temper his doubts found their outlet.

A week after their homecoming, Cuin noted Ellid wandering all alone toward the Forest. Frowning, he hurried after her; it was not the first time she had broken bounds of late.

"You should not go out alone, Ellid," he said sharply when he had caught up with her.

"I am not afraid," she answered, though with none of her former fire in her voice.

"And what of me? I am in charge of you until your father returns. If any ill should come to you, he will flay me." Cuin stood staring at her, tight-lipped with exasperation. He knew she was un-happy; nothing but misery could make Ellid so tame. He would far rather she would weep out-right than face him so silently. His love for her nearly choked him.

"If you would walk," he said gruffly at last, "I will get Flessa and come with you."

Flessa was Cuin's falcon. A shade of a smile moved Ellid's still lips, for she knew that Cuin had better things to do than go a-hawking with such poor company. But he saw that smile as a light in the wilderness. "Wait but a moment," he exclaimed, and ran to fetch the bird.

They roamed along the fringes of the Forest. They scarcely spoke, but Cuin was content that she walked at his side. Rabbits were feeding in the grass beneath the trees. Twice Cuin unhooded the flame-red falcon and loosed it, and it returned faithfully with the game each time. But the third time it swerved from its course like a spark caught in the wind and shot away toward the treetops.

Cuin gave a cry of anger and sorrow; many hours of patient work were in the training of that bird. "Stay here—nay, go back!" he told Ellid, and plunged after it amongst the trees. But Ellid was one, like her cousin, who took direction ill. "I am coming," she retorted, and entered the Forest on his heels.

They struggled along in panting haste. Soon they saw the falcon sitting high in a tall pine, bright as fire in the sunlight. Cuin whistled and swung the lure, but the bird flashed away forthwith toward the denser cover. Cuin muttered to himself. A deep ravine interrupted the way. They scrambled down quickly and toiled up the opposite slope, hoisting themselves by their hands. Then Cuin gasped and almost fell. A white hart leaped to the bank just above, leaped again and vanished.

Ellid sprang to where it had stood like one who has sprouted wings. "Bevan?" she cried in a voice like larksong. Struggling below, Cuin heard the soft answering call: "Here." When Cuin came to his feet, he found the black-haired stranger standing beneath a silver beech, and the lady kissing him—such a kiss as Cuin had never known from her.

"We do your cousin discourtesy," Bevan said to her gently when he could speak.

"Cuin!" Ellid exclaimed, and reached out to the silent watcher. But Cuin turned away from her outstretched hand. "I will wait," he mumbled and strode off blindly, his bird forgotten.

"We have grieved him," Ellid said sorrowfully. "But I have grieved him aplenty this fortnight past. Now he knows the reason."

The two sat and talked for a time. Bevan told her much news, even of the Speaking Stone. "It is a hard saying, that I may not look upon the sea," he mourned.

Ellid glanced at him askance. To her, as to most folk, the sea was a name of horror. Ages past, it was said, the gods had driven monstrous beings from the face of the land, and the dark waves of the flood teemed with them yet. The huge dragon that ruled the deep, folk said, was grown so great that all of Isle would make but a stepping-place for his clawed foot. If ever he should arise. . . . Ellid shuddered, but then recalled that she had also once feared the night.

"I wish I could have taken the silver sea-drake back to her proper abode for her rest," Bevan said. "But your father honored her well. When I left they were raising great barrows for her and for the slain. Myrdon will be leveled when they are done."

"Isle will be well rid of it," Ellid replied. "That was a stronghold fit for nothing but war and uses of war. My father has no desire of such."

Bevan's delicate mouth quirked, for he did not have such a high opinion of her father. "It may be I shall not see you now a while," he told her obliquely.

"Why?" she asked, startled.

He hardly knew why, what peril pursued him or what call drew him, but he felt he must travel. "I do not like the rising sun," he answered lightly. "It seems to me that I must follow the setting sun a while. Now that I have the steeds, I can better learn to know this strange land of men."

Ellid was puzzled but said no more. Bevan kissed her deeply and arose. "Come," he said. "We must go to Cuin, though he will give us cold welcome."

They found him sitting not far away. Bevan squatted before him. "I did not think to affront you thus, my lord," he told him quietly. "When I lured you off, I never guessed that the lady would follow. Though I should have known she might."

Cuin raised his head slowly to stare. "Lured me? What do you mean?"

Bevan called, a strange call, and raised his wrist. The falcon appeared with blazing speed to his summons. Even Cuin winced as the talons drove at Bevan's white flesh, but Flessa alighted gently and folded her shining wings. Bevan held her up before his face, studying her, the golden blinking eyes scarcely inches from his own.

Then he handed her back onto Cuin's leathern sleeve. "She would have returned to you unsummoned," he told him. "You need no leash or hood to constrain her to cleave to you, Cuin son of Clarric the Wise."

Cuin only eyed him coldly for reply and rose to stand at Ellid's side. "Come, Cousin."

"The blessing of the Mothers go with you, my lady," Bevan called softly as they walked away. When Ellid turned to look, he was gone. Not even a footfall could be heard to mark his going.

Ellid and Cuin walked in silence until they reached the meadow. "I am sorry that I could not tell you," she said at last. "I love him well, Cuin."

"Yet I have stood by you these many years," he said roughly.

"You are my good and faithful friend, Cuin. Pray stand by me still. No one must know of this."

Cuin was ready to burst with anguish and vexation, but still he could not refuse her request. "Even so," he promised heavily at last. "But will

you tell me what he is, Ellid, that you tender him
your regard?"

"He is what you have seen," she replied with
eyes wide and bright as sunlit skies. "He is master
of bird and beast and all things of earth."

Cuin only glowered for answer, and left her at
the gates. He climbed to his comfortless chamber,
where he hooded his bird and leashed her to her
perch. Then he sat with blood-red jealousy color-
ing his sight. How could Ellid prefer such a
beardless beggar over him! But Cuin did not weep
for the loss of his lady, for he deemed he was
not bested yet, and he was far from ready to quit
the field. Cuin was the son of one titled Wise, and
though he did not yet know his father's serenity,
he had learned the value of tenacity. He would
stay by his lady's side; when she needed him, he
would be there. Perhaps she would yet find that
her old love could serve her the better.

Cuin set his straight jaw as he set his course,
and his rugged, fighter's face went hard as rock.
His was to be a silent perseverance. He suffered
by the warrior's code, and he never thought to
woo his lady with the ardor that burned his heart.

The news that Dacaerin's men brought back
from Myrdon did nothing to ease Cuin's wrath:
silver dragons, forsooth, and speaking stones! He
could only think that he had some trickster warlock for a rival, and he boiled inwardly at the mention of him. Moreover, Pryce Dacaerin seemed to
be as much taken by Bevan as Ellid herself, and
as much cooled toward Cuin. His wife, Eitha, a
comely, peace-loving woman, went about her work
with a puzzled frown. Cuin held his tongue,
curbed his temper and bided his time. He saw

Ellid as often as he could, if only to sit with her, walk by her side, bid her good day. . . . And as for Ellid; she dreamed.

It was the beginning of June when the dark men came, a dozen in a troop. Dacaerin would refuse hospitality to no travelers, though he did not like the looks of these folk who went close-cloaked even in the warmth of summer. Their leader was one who called himself Ware, an emissary of some unfamiliar southern lord who sought the newcome heir of Byve to "do him honor." To this one Dacaerin replied honestly that he had not seen Bevan in nearly a month and did not know where he might be. Ellid and Cuin kept silence. Though the swarthy strangers tried hard to be pleasant, something about them spoke so loudly of peril that even the servant-folk shied from them. There was small doubt in Cuin's mind as to what sort of "honor" they wished to pay Bevan.

They stayed for several days, lazing about and listening at doors. As each day passed, Cuin became harder pressed to maintain his disinterested courtesy. He believed he knew where Bevan was to be found, for he read Ellid like a weathercock; never had he known her to take such an interest in sunsets. And though Cuin knew that he could not betray Bevan to these dark folk without hurting Ellid to her core, still the thought pricked at him: how sweet a way to be rid of his rival! The niggling desire, so alien to his stalwart nature, pestered him almost to distraction. The sight of a cloaked visitor became poison to him; he dodged them as if they were pox-ridden. But it seemed that they were everywhere. "Enough!" Cuin cried to himself on the fifth day. "I will go to my father's house and leave this den of madness."

In haste, without provisions or farewells, he
mounted his horse and sent it swiftly toward his
family's estate of Wallyn that lay a week's journey
to the west. But, once out of sight of Caer Eitha,
he slackened his pace. It would scarcely avail him
to lame his horse with days of travel before him.
The track, like all tracks he knew, lay through
the ancient Forest that cloaked all the land between men's puny sunlit strongholds. The old
trees were tall and thick with all sorts of clinging
growth. They shadowed the road so that it ran
like a tunnel, lost in gloom to front and rear.
Cuin went warily and more than warily, mutter-
ing at himself for hearing noises. He had traveled
this way before; it was not as if he were a callow
novice. . . . !

Within an hour the cloaked riders came at him
out of the gloom to the rear. Cuin rounded on
them and drew his sword, but they were eight to
his one; he could not kill any, or even draw blood,
though some of his blows struck home. They dis-
armed him deftly and hurried him away from the
road. Presently they came to a clear circular dingle around a giant oak, and there they stopped.

"Now," demanded one whom Cuin knew as
Rebd, "where is he?"

"Where is who?" Cuin demanded in turn.

"He whom you go to meet! Is it for pleasure
that you ride beneath the woven shade? Where is
the black-haired Prince?"

"I ride toward Wallyn," Cuin replied, furious
that he must explain his business to such as these.
But the cloaked men barked with cold laughter.

"Without so much as a crust?" retorted Rebd.
"Come, my young lord, tell us where he bides.

Consider that we will have it out of you soon enough."

"By my troth," Cuin flared at the threat, "you shall have nothing from me except my curse and the sharp point of my sword when next we meet!" But the cloaked men laughed at this, also.

"He who is sacrificed at the oak cannot curse the priests of the mantled god. Indeed, you will be one of our number this day unless you tell us what we need to know."

Cuin stared speechlessly. He could put the bold face to pain and loss of life; these were things he had been reared to endure. But Rebd spoke of an evil he had thought long gone from the world of men.

"Tell us of Byve's heir," Rebd commanded.

"I have nothing to tell you," Cuin muttered. What could he say to them? Not for any hatred would he deliver Bevan over to such as these. If they should find that Ellid held him dear! Cuin would have died rather than so endanger her, but not even the mercy of death was to be his lot, it seemed.

The cloaked men held Cuin and stripped him to the waist. Their hands were cold like fish on his flesh; he shuddered from their touch. They tied his wrists and strung him up to a limb of the ancient oak. They kindled fire before his dangling feet.

Think of Ellid, he charged himself.

They heated their sword blades in the fire and seared him with the flats, drawing them slowly over his chest in the shape of ancient runes of evil. Their dun-gray faces were the faces of corpses beneath their hoods.

Think of Ellid, fair as a falcon in the sunlight.

*These will make of me a thing she would flee in
terror and loathing. . . . No matter, as long as
they touch her not. Think of Ellid.*

"The oak has need of blood," Rebd said.

They switched their cooling swords to the blade
and traced the loops of his ribs with the points.
Warm trickles of his blood splattered to the leaf-
mold below. Rebd swung Cuin around like so
much meat and slashed a shallow circle just
below his straining shoulder blades.

Think of Ellid and say no word—

"Son of Clarric," Rebd remarked, "we will let
you know what sort of a thing you will be when
you render service to the lord of the oak." He
went to throw off his cloak, and for the first time
Cuin cried out and turned away his face; he could
not bear to see. *Let them tear the heart from him
if they would, but to look on one who walked the
land without it. . . .*

"Tell us of the son of Byve, lordling."

"I have nothing to say to you," Cuin whispered
with averted eyes.

"Then must we hang your heart from the oaken
bole."

Cuin heard them coming; he tightened himself
against them as he tightened his eyes against the
sight of them. *Think of Ellid*—but his thoughts
were interrupted by a voice soft and startling as a
cat's leap.

"You seek me, servants of the mantled lord?"

Cuin's eyes flew open. Rebd was before him, a
shape of horror, indeed, but Cuin's sight moved
beyond him and the others to where Bevan sat
his steed with drawn sword. Even as Rebd whirled
to face him, he sent his horse plunging into the
hollow. To Cuin's dazzled sight it seemed that

Bevan shone with white fire. He charged through the cloaked priests of Pel before they could move to prevent him, and he freed Cuin with a mere touch to the rope. The dark men set upon Bevan then. He swung at them with his sword that flickered with pale flame. Terror of him seemed to work upon them; they shrank from before his clumsy strokes. But they came at him from behind, and Cuin did not see how he could prevail.

Sudden strength of rage ran through Cuin. Shouting, he pulled a brand from the fire and thrust it full into that thing he had not been able to face: the dark, unhealing cavern that was Rebd's back. Rebd screamed and fell. Cuin seized his sword and flung himself at the others, frenzied at the memory of his own blood. Two he skewered, and Bevan or his steed had felled two more when the remaining three lost their nerve and fled on foot behind their bolting horses.

Without a word Bevan leaned down and beheaded those who lay in the dingle. Cuin could have stood the sight of their blood, but it shook him that there was none. Dizzily he clung to the rough trunk of the oak, and then he slipped down to lie at its roots. He saw Bevan leave the hollow, riding hard after dark, scurrying figures. Then he thought of Rebd, and fainted.

He awoke to the touch of cool water. He found himself sitting against the oak, a blanket padding his wounded back, and Bevan kneeling before him bathing his cuts and burns. The water floated thick with herbs, Cuin noted, and there seemed to be some healing virtue to it. Already the pain of his hurts grew less. But beyond Bevan lay the still and headless form of something less than man. Cuin closed his eyes as sickness seized him.

He heard Bevan moving about, then felt the stem
of a flask between his teeth. He gulped, and found
the liquor as potent as any he had ever tasted.
When he looked again, Rebd's body was cloaked
like the others.

"What goes here, my lord Cuin?" Bevan asked
quietly. "Tell me not my lady is in peril from such
as these."

"There are four more like this at the fortress,"
Cuin muttered wearily, "but she was well when
I left."

"What, then, did she send you to me? Surely
she knew you would be followed."

"Nay, I am here of my own accord." Cuin met
his eyes candidly. "You must know that I have
borne you small love, lord. When these dark folk
were forever asking for you, it galled me to distraction that I could not with honor oblige them.
. . . So like a fool I set flight willy-nilly toward my
father's house, thinking only to escape hearing
your name for a while. But these quaintly thought
that I was your friend."

"I wish you were, Cuin son of Clarric," Bevan
said softly. "Indeed, you have befriended me well
this day. But small wonder that you hate me. I
have reft from you your birthright, she who is of
all things most precious."

"You have taken from me nothing that I ever
owned," Cuin replied heavily, though he could
not have told where he had got that knowledge.

"That was well said." Bevan regarded him
gravely. "In very sooth she is as free as the wind.
No man can own her."

Bevan tore strips of bandaging from his old
shirt. He padded Cuin's wounds and wrapped
them tightly to stay their sluggish bleeding. Once

done, he wordlessly fetched Cuin's shirt and tunic.

"Is there a place hereabouts," Cuin asked him, "where I can lie hidden? I have not strength now to ride to Wallyn."

Bevan eyed him quizzically. "Think, my lord: Why did I ride after those unmade men of the mantled lord? I have neither talent nor taste for killing even such as these. Yet all are silenced, and you can return to Caer Eitha at once. Indeed, return you must, unless you would henceforth be pursued by these cloaked priests of Pel."

Cuin gulped as Bevan's words struck in. If he became quarry for these dark hunters he would never with safety see Ellid or home again. "I must put the bold face to them," he muttered.

"Even so." Bevan was using his water to wash the blood from below the tree. He hid the rope and scattered the ashes of the fire. "If it is any comfort," he added as he worked, "I think they can but slay you, not unmake you as they threatened to do into a heartless one like them. Only Pel has that power. It is strange how a good thing can come to evil use. The golden vessel which gifted the gods with endless youth now quickens the sinews of these poor mutilated things."

"So unless they come at me with a pot, I need fear only mortal destruction, hah?" Cuin rose stiffly to his feet, but swayed before he could mount his steed. Bevan handed him the flask.

"Let them think you are drunk. For the matter of that, a few more pulls and you will be. But if it comes to fighting, my lord, remember that they can only be stunned by a body blow, not destroyed."

"Between heart and head, only head is left to

slay them by. I undertand." Cuin pulled himself
onto his steed and sat with reasonable steadiness.
"I must be off while I am able."

"Let your gods lend you strength. And lord . . ."
—Bevan hesitated— ". . . tender my greeting to
my lady, if you will."

"It would have been done without your asking."
Cuin stayed a moment longer and wordlessly extended his hand; Bevan grasped it. "For my life
I thank you, my lord," Cuin muttered, and
wheeled his horse away before Bevan could reply.
Bevan watched him go, a straight-lipped, stiff-
backed young warrior on a fine roan horse. Then
he sighed and set himself to hiding the bodies.

CHAPTER SIX

Ellid had not seen Cuin leāve, nor the band of cloaked riders. But waiting for the sunset as was her custom, she saw Cuin return, and she knew at once that something was amiss. Never had she seen him ride so recklessly or leave his horse so unheedingly to another's care. In the great hall below, she knew, sat her father with that putty-faced Ware; not that he bore him any love, but the fellow was a guest. Swiftly Ellid went to speak to Cuin before he blundered in on them.

She was too late. Even as she reached the door Cuin swaggered through, brandishing his flask, and greeted his uncle with an expansive courtesy. Pryce Dacaerin glared at him, for he brooked no license in his troops or his household. "What do you mean, sir?"

"I have found ā tree," Cuin replied lucidly. "Lovely tree. Make my home there someday—"

Pryce sputtered speechlessly, but Ware came to his feet. "My young lord of Wallyn, did you meet with men of mine in the Forest?"

"Forest?" Cuin ogled vaguely. "Aye, there was a Forest, I dare say, but I spent the day with my tree. Eyes for none other. Leaves like lips for softness, bole round as a woman's butt—"

"Get to your chamber, sirrah!" Dacaerin roared. Ellid stiffened where she stood by the door, but not because of what Cuin had said. On his back, where he stood between her and the others, she spied a spreading blossom of bright red. Quickly she went to him and put her arm around him tenderly, hiding the bloodspot with her hand.

"It is my fault, Father," she said regretfully. "I have been cool to him of late, and it has driven him to dishonor." Steadily she met her father's enraged eyes. "I will take him in hand," she said. "Come, Cuin." Gently she led him from the room, supporting him with her encircling arm. She whispered to him the while, and little did the others guess that it was not endearments she told him.

She got him to his chamber and, pale with shock, made as if to examine the wound. Cuin stopped her. "They might yet come sneaking this way," he told her. "I must yet be a drunk and lie on my back, hah?"

"Be easy," she replied, looking out the window-slot. "There they go, all four of them."

The cloaked visitors had taken to the Forest to seek their missing comrades, and in a minute Pryce Dacaerin appeared at the chamber door, still blustering. "Now hear me well, both of you!" he shouted, but stopped when he saw Cuin's blood spotting the straw.

"I am no drunkard, Uncle," Cuin muttered, and toppled into a faint deep as any drunken stupor. Ellid and her father got the shirt off him and dressed his wounds, but they had no more speech from him that day.

Cuin awoke to first daylight the next morning and at once steeled himself to rise. But he need not have troubled; the cloaked men had not returned. Nor did they come that day or on those that followed. On the fifth day, in sheerest curiosity, Pryce Dacaerin took a troop and spent the day in the Forest. But no sign of them did he find.

Cuin stayed at Caer Eitha until the middle of June, when his wounds were mostly healed and his strength returned. Then he went to Ellid. A quaint trouble was in his heart now that he could no longer hate his rival.

"Small wonder that you cleave to him," he told her wearily. "Though he is no warrior, he is much man."

"He is more than man. The blood of the Mother Goddess is in him." Ellid could not have said why she told Cuin what she had carefully kept from everyone else. "He was born of Celonwy after she had helped Byve from the burning towers of Eburacon. It is but lately that he has left the hollow hills of his kin."

"And the Stone hailed him. And now that blood-fed lord who smote down his father seeks him also. But chance he shall be a match for him." Cuin rose. "I wish him victory, Cousin, and you the joy of his victory. I will go to my father's house now. May I be of better use there."

She rose speechlessly to stand beside him. "Go carefully," she said at last.

"I will take some manservants with me." He stood looking at her, and in spite of all his resolve his heart ached. "Kiss me but once, Ellid," he requested quietly, "for friendship."

"For friendship, ay," she agreed hesitantly, and kissed him gently on the lips. Cuin went then without facing her again. But had he known it, her eyes followed him with better regard than she had given him in many weeks past.

When he was packed and provisioned, Cuin went finally to the chamber where Flessa sat hooded and leashed to her perch. He took her up on his unprotected arm, for he was indifferent to a few more slashes now. "Free as the wind, he called my lady," Cuin muttered. "Truly I can put no claim on the wind; nor shall I put any on you, flying thing. Let you be another free as the wind. Go and find yourself a sweetheart, if you will." He carried the falcon to the courtyard, unhooded her and let her take wing. Joyously the bird circled away, flickering like a flame in the sunlight. But as Cuin mounted and rode out of the gate, Flessa appeared with blazing quickness and startled him by alighting on his shoulder.

For miles her warm wing caressed his ear. Throughout the seven days' ride to Wallyn she stayed with him, sometimes speeding ahead and waiting in the roadside trees, sometimes perched sedately on his pack animal or his wrist. Cuin's men smiled among themselves in wonder at her, and Cuin himself felt his heart lighten because of her faithfulness. When they came to Wallyn at last, Flessa entered the gate fearlessly and settled herself on the orchard wall, where no one dared disturb her.

Wallyn was a gentle place, more walled garden than fortress, an oddity in that time as Eburacon

had been in times past. Clarric of Wallyn was an
oddity also, a man who took more kindly to books
than to battle. Mean-hearted folk sniggered that
the lady Rayna had married him to have her way
with him, for till her death she had been as fiery
and willful as her brother Pryce. Yet many lords
respected Clarric for his gentle mind that still
would cut its way to sooth like a sword. And Cuin,
like others who knew him well, deemed that his
father lacked no strength of spirit.

"You do not look well in heart, lad," Clarric
greeted his son.

"Strange events are going forward, Father,"
Cuin replied, "and I have need of your counsel.
Have you heard anything of cloaked riders, or of
the black-haired heir of Byve?"

"Whispers," Clarric told him. "But I see now
that your body is as sore as the rest of you. Bathe
now, and eat. Talk will go better later."

Indeed, they talked late into the night. It took
Cuin that long to voice the sharpest perplexity
that rankled him. "All the world knows that I
love Ellid," he said painfully, "and all the world
says that what a man desires he must grasp and
take, if he is truly to be a man; that is a warrior's
way. But I feel of late that I have no right to
constrain her with even so much as the sight of
my saddened face. It is very strange."

"Not so strange," Clarric mused. "I would say
that you have learned to love better than one who
would reach and grasp. I would say also that
perhaps family is at fault here for having thrust
you two so much together. This Bevan who claims
kinship with the gods; perhaps she is his by a
right greater than your birthright. Surely she is
worthy of his regard. Think on it, my son."

"He is an uncommon one, that is sure," Cuin sighed. "For little as I know him, I can feel his stature, he who looks to be no more than a youth. . . . And I cannot hate him. If it were not such a wrench, I believe that I could almost admire him." Cuin laughed, and Clarric laughed with him, glad that his son still could make light of his heartache. For this matter of Ellid, Clarric knew that there was nothing he could do except what comes hardest to a father: listen and wait. And for some few weeks, he resolved, he would not burden his son with much work. Cuin looked worn from wounds as well as from sorrow.

So it was, a few days later, that Cuin was doing nothing more strenuous than polishing his helm when a servant reported someone that in the courtyard wished to speak with him.

"Who?" demanded Cuin, as a lingering dread of the dark priests of Pel pricked his mind.

" 'Pon my word, master, I do not know! 'Tis a black-haired youth, no more, but yet I half-fear him. His eyes burned through me."

"Bevan?" Cuin exclaimed, and ran below. It was Bevan indeed, looking slight as a boy among the huskier men of the keep. Cuin found himself smiling to see him.

"By the Mothers, you turn up everywhere," he greeted him. "How did you know I was home?"

Bevan nodded at the falcon, who even then was aiming herself at Cuin's arm. "I knew it when I saw the bird, not before. I hoped only to work a trade of horses. But it would have been scant courtesy to have passed this way without giving you greeting, my lord. Are you well?"

"Well enough. Pray come within, lord Bevan; my father will be eager to meet you."

Bevan led his horse gently to the stable, for it was very lame. Then he and Cuin went to where Clarric sat stooped over his accounts. The older man left his work gladly to talk with them. By evening Bevan was speaking to the scholar and his son more openly than he had ever spoken to Pryce Dacaerin.

"I showed myself to those last four priests of Pel," he explained, "and led them a few days' jaunt to the north to get them out of the way. I summoned up a shade at last to rid me of them; strange that they who are themselves but living dead should have such horror of the bodiless dead. But I lost one horse to the chase, and now I have lamed the other. Wallyn is a place of fair repute, so I did not fear to come here and bargain for a fresh mount. I would be content to go afoot, for I can go as well afoot as most men on a horse. But to fight these servants of the mantled lord I must be mounted."

"So you will fight them," Cuin said.

"Ay, by all that is dark and beautiful, what else? I cannot run from them forever." Bevan sighed. "Though I scarcely thought, when I came to this world of men, to battle for my father's kingdom. Revenge, honor, blood-price and face-price; these are words without meaning beneath the hollow hills. But now that I have seen how men feed on fear and blood. . . ." He grimaced. "Does it seem likely to you, lord of Wallyn, that further strife can put an end to it?"

"No man can speak for men," Clarric answered quietly. "The riddle is useless, Bevan of Eburacon, for what choice do you have? The Stone has spoken, and Pel Blagden has heard."

Bevan winced. "Ay, even so. Already the word

of the Forest is that fire is seen again in that Pit
far to the south. Pel Blagden seeks to augment his
army by the vile means you know, Cuin—means
he has not troubled to practice these hundred
years or more. After the fall of Eburacon he still
had servants enough for his purpose."

"Do they never die?" Cuin exclaimed.

"Never, unless they are slain by the sword, by
beheading."

"So how will you slay them, then, Bevan?"
Cuin asked dryly. "I dare say you are skilled in
many weapons, but surely the sword is not one of
them."

Bevan faced him with a trace of a smile. "I
would be lessoned by you, my lord, but it would
be perilous for me to stay so long. Yet surely there
are folk in Isle who will lend their swords to my
aid if they can be made to see the peril. I must
seek them out."

"You shall have my aid and that of my folk,"
Clarric told him. "Though we are no great warriors here, except Cuin."

"And as for that," Cuin added, "you shall be
lessoned yet if I have my way. Let me go with
you, Bevan." He could not believe the words he
heard himself saying.

Bevan was as astonished as he, if he could
judge that ever-sober face. But there was something more than astonishment; maybe a touch of
joy? "Think well, Cuin," Bevan said after a pause.
"Are you so ready to face them again?"

"Soon or late, face them I must." Cuin turned
to Clarric. "Father?"

"Sleep on it, lad," Clarric said heavily. "My lord
Bevan, will you not sup with us, and lie in a bed
this night?"

"I will sup with you gladly," Bevan replied, "but I take better comfort in the Forest than in any roof of man, even one as fair as this." He paused. "Cuin, if you would ride with me indeed, I—I shall be well content. But you must consider, as your father has said. I will wait on you in the morning."

"Nay," Cuin answered, "I will go with you when we have eaten." And his father did not gainsay him.

They left in the twilight dimness, a strange hour for Cuin to start a journey, but the best of hours for Bevan. The heir of Byve rode a fine steed of dapple-gray, the best in Clarric's stables. Cuin rode his favorite roan. No sooner was he mounted than Flessa flew down to take her place on his shoulder.

They rode to the end of the tilled land in a silence that spoke more than words. Scarcely had they entered the deeper shadows of the Forest than Cuin espied a flash of white between the trees. *Ghost!* his mind screamed, but his eyes looked again; it was the figure of a white hart that ran beside them, of which the Speaking Stone had told.

BOOK TWO:
THE SIX SOULS

Whither goes the white stag
And the falcon red?
Cuin, Cuin Clarric's son,
Whither are you led?

Whither goes the dusky gray
And the russet roan?
Bevan of Eburacon
Walks no more alone.

Walks no more alone, and yet
What man knows his heart?
What woman knows his inwardness
Who walked so long apart?

Hawk-red roan and dapple-gray,
The falcon and the hart;
Bevan of Eburacon
Is served by Cuin Kellarth.

CHAPTER ONE

Within a few days Cuin had discovered that Bevan had strength disproportionate to his slight build, grace and quickness like a cat, and surpassingly dexterous hands. Yet he took poorly to the swordsmanship.

"You have need of a better weapon," Cuin excused him. Bevan's sword was heavy, ancient and battered; indeed, to Cuin's shock, he used it for cutting firewood.

"If I am meant to go on with this struggle, one will come to me." Over the flickering campfire, Bevan's sober face was unreadable. "That will be a sweet proving. It is hard for me to feel surely that I take the right path, Cuin. Before I came to this strange world of men, what was right was what came gently to my hand. Which this fighting skill does no whit."

"It is a skill which requires much training," Cuin replied, "even among those who do it best."

Bevan eyed him askance. "Bloodletting does not come easily, then, even to the hands of evil men? Then least of all should it have come to you, Cuin. I warrant you got it not at your father's house."

Cuin smiled wryly. "Nay, my uncle taught me. But it is a needful learning in these times, Bevan, and one which my father does not scorn. Many times has my uncle's might defended the gentler folk of Wallyn. Pryce Dacaerin's reach is long."

"You were reared by him."

"Ay, since my tenth winter. As befits his heir."

"You are much like him." Bevan regarded Cuin steadily. "Yet I believe you are more like your father."

"Pryce Dacaerin is a valiant man, and worthy of my service," Cuin said quietly. "Yet I am proud to be my father's son."

They traveled softly southward, keeping to the west but within the rim of the hills that rose between Isle and the sea. To the eyes of men they were two, the slender black-haired youth and the clear-eyed young warrior at his side. But to Bevan's way of thinking they were six who journeyed through the dim Forest. Two were men and two were swift steeds and two were even more fleeting things, the flame-red bird and the subtle white deer.

"How did you come by this hart?" Cuin asked, and Bevan could not answer. He could not say that he had seen it first on the day he rescued Ellid. By unspoken accord they did not mention her.

"You have heard that it is laid as a destiny on me," he said at last.

"Ay, by the Stone. And this falcon: Was it laid a destiny on me by a certain son of the immortals?"

Bevan smiled faintly. "You overdeem me, Cuin son of Clarric. I spoke but what I saw. It may be

that we all have some soul that cleaves to us, for
good or for ill."

Their course meandered with the crumpled
land and the crooked Forest tracks. From time to
time they came to various holdings, each a sunlit
patch amidst the surrounding shade. Centered, as
if shrinking from the trees, would be a stronghold.
Some were round towers such as Myrdon had
been. Some were squat walls and ditches. Some
were stone and most were wood. All were tense,
watching walls, suspicious and threatening at the
same time.

Cuin knew many of these local lords. Often
they had dealings with Pryce Dacaerin, bartering
for his favor and his aid against whatever threat
might loom at the time. Some were of greater in-
fluence than others. To their great halls Cuin and
Bevan would ride boldly, gaining news and a sup
and a cautious promise of aid in times to come.
Bevan knew that they vouchsafed their hospitality and their word for the sake of Dacaerin's heir,
not for him. Though they had heard of the
cloaked riders roaming the land, their fear was
not yet strong. Blagden, that dark place of horrors,
was far away. And long since faded from memory
were the days when only tribute of bright gold
bought escape from the bloodstained oak.

The two travelers always returned to the Forest
to sleep, or rather for Cuin to sleep and Bevan to
roam. Bevan would be pent under no roof after
dark.

"We have marked ourselves with these visits,"
Cuin said over the fire one night. "We should be
pursued."

"The Forest night is full of voices which con-
spire to protect us," Bevan replied. "Be easy,

Cuin." But Cuin noted that Bevan was more wary
in the weeks that followed. He led them on some
strange paths; indeed, their trail was as tortuous
as a bat's. Moreover, at times they took refuge in
the thickest cover, silent for hours at a stretch.
Cuin did not know what sense or informant
warned Bevan of peril, but he saw proof of their
pursuers. One day Bevan turned hastily aside
from the Forest track and motioned Cuin behind
a line of tall thorns. He held the horses' heads;
the beasts stood still as stone while Cuin peered
out beneath the branches and watched the priests
of Pel ride by.

Then Bevan took them on another crazy turn
toward the setting sun. Still, they made their way
mostly southward, far beyond the "long reach" of
Pryce Dacaerin and beyond any lands that Cuin
had knowledge of—until one day that was not yet
mid-summer they came to the end of the trees.

Cuin gaped like a boy. He had never known
that a sky could stretch so wide. Before him rolled
the sunlit folds of the South Downs. Waist-tall
grass flowed in waves beneath the wind like nothing that either of them had ever seen. A towering
elm on the farthest rise seemed but a sapling in
the shimmering expanse.

"The hart will not follow us there," Bevan said
bleakly.

Cuin glanced at him curiously. It was seldom
enough that the white hart followed them any-
where. More often it dashed off upon its own in-
scrutable errands. They were likely not to see it
for days at a time. But this day it was close at
hand, standing not a furlong away, with its silver-
crowned head raised high to survey the strange
terrain.

For his own part, Cuin felt an unreasoning lift of heart at the sight of so much sunny sky. But he understood why Bevan looked grim, or so he thought; it would be dangerous to venture out upon those shelterless meadows. "Still there's nothing else for it," Bevan muttered and dismounted. He strode to the deer and spoke to it, and it whirled and darted away amongst the trees.

"He will await us at Eburacon," Bevan told Cuin, and rode away from the Forest without a glance. They traveled the rolling land, five souls now, until darkness spread its petals in the vast dome of the sky. Cuin had never seen such a soft blossoming of the dusky flower of night. He was almost glad that Bevan pushed on beneath its star-flecked blackness. In these wide, shadowless lands, the pale light of the young moon made plain the way even to Cuin's unaccustomed eyes. It was late when they stopped, and Cuin did not need the comfort of a fire to send him sleep.

In the morning he realized that these curving Downs were in fact the gentlest mountain that he had ever known. They were camped on its rounded peak, and far away to the east it billowed until its folds were blurred with distance. To the west the drop was steeper, though no less soft, and at its base ran a bright river of silver that curved away into the shadows of wooded hills.

"Beyond yon Gleaming River lies the kingdom of Welas," Bevan said.

There, Cuin knew, lived strange, dark folk who spoke their own unintelligible tongue. He glanced apprehensively, but Bevan turned from the westward view with a sigh.

"Our business does not lie there," he told Cuin,

"but to the east. From now on we travel by night." He squinted painfully into the blaze of the rising sun.

That way lay Blagden Pit, a place strong men chose not to muse on overmuch. To venture even onto the marches of that demesne was foolhardy. Yet, with the perverse pride of one who has embraced the servant's role, Cuin scorned to ask Bevan his plans for those dread parts. In his war-trained mind he supposed that the Prince sought a look at the lay of the land, a quick and covert sortie. That was peril enough, but Cuin shrugged the thought from him. Shadows of Blagden had no place in this high skylit land.

They spent the day nestled in a dimple of the Downs, taking watch by turns. The horses bloated themselves upon the long sweet grass, and Flessa brought rabbits until they bade her stop. Cuin dozed in the sunshine and listened to the singing of countless laverocs, or larks. He could not feel foreboding in so lovely a place, however different it was from anything he had known. When twilight came, scarcely softer than the day of bright haze and rippling breeze, he mounted his roan and followed Bevan contentedly.

For a fortnight of nights they traveled. By degrees the high, rolling land lowered and leveled until they were riding across a featureless plain. Cuin's serenity left him, for they were hard pressed to find cover. Every day they spent in fear of enemy eyes. Wherever they camped, whether in the lee of some sparse hedgerow or behind a byre, they could see the priests of Pel scurrying antlike along the nameless tracks that traced the plain. Hooded gore-crows flapped above, their sight sharp to every movement on their dark lord's domain. Cuin cringed lest one of them should be Pel himself, for with his ancient powers of will he could take on what form or delusion he chose; all mortal sight bent to his command.

Still, nothing went wrong for Bevan and Cuin. On the thirteenth day they sighted thick black puffs of smoke on the horizon and knew that they were near the Pit. That night they made Blagden, and no watcher sounded an alarm. Cuin could not believe that they were unseen. All his senses screamed of a trap yet to be sprung as they rode to the edge in the plain light of a full moon.

Blagden Pit was a gaping hole in the level green plain—a sinister place even to think of, for how had it come there? Only sorcery could have dug such a den without raising great dikes of earth. At the very base of the pit, a mile below the vast rim, was a stronghold set into the stony flanks of the chasm like a plug in a twisted funnel. Down to it ran a crooked track, through gates at the rim and gates below; a horse could descend that way if it were bold and sure of foot. But no horse could reach Blagden fortress without passing the gates. Bevan dismounted and gave Cuin his reins.

"You cannot be serious!" Cuin whispered. "What can you hope to gain!"

"That is as it comes," Bevan murmured. "Perhaps no more than knowledge."

"If you go there, you'll go without me! Not for any knowledge, gold or fame would I venture into that pit. Likely it is the gate of hell itself, and fire burns beyond the door!" Dread of the place drenched Cuin and filled him like fog; he shook with the chill of it. But Bevan faced him without comment.

"Nay, you must keep the horses," he said placidly. "Seek cover to the north and let Flessa lead me to you. Farewell." As Cuin only stared in anguish, he frowned, puzzled. "What is the matter, Cuin? You know I move like a shade in the night."

"Even so," Cuin muttered. "Farewell." And he rode hastily away. He made a wide detour around the Pit and found concealment in a deserted cottage on the farther side. Folk did not care to live near the place, it seemed, and Cuin himself would rather have been far from it. Anger at Bevan and at his own cowardice tied him in knots; he could not eat or sleep. The constant harsh talk of the gore-crows jeered him. He paced away the night and the next day, and started at every shadow, but Bevan did not come.

He had been caught by the dawn, Cuin told himself, and was loath to move about in daylight. But when the next night was half-spent, Cuin could no longer argue that all might yet be well. He broke camp and rode slowly around the rim of Blagden Pit, desperate for some sign of reassurance. None came. At last Cuin tethered the horses to the northward and, faint with fear, started down the steep and barren slope toward the darkest shadow of that darkened place.

There were guards about, here and there. Cuin avoided them almost impatiently. He reached the depth at last and recklessly scaled the wall. The gloom was so dense that he expected he would blunder into a sentry before he ever saw him. But he met no one as he dropped within and felt

his way to the keep. Then, as he rounded a corner
of the hulking mass of stone, the gloom gave way
to a red glare. Cuin discovered that he would have
no trouble finding Bevan.

Several hundred men were facing the fire: unmade men, rather, the servants of the mantled
lord. Their cloaked backs were ranged toward
Cuin, and his vision shot beyond them. Over a
pulsing-hot mass of coals hung a huge basin
which pierced the dark with its red-gold gleam.
Above it loomed a giant oak, the only tree in Pel's
barren pit, a goodly growing thing that was rendered a vile presence in this baleful place. Dark,
flapping forms clustered on its branches and circled greedily near the fire. A tall hooded figure
loomed like the oak beside the caldron, reddened
with its glow. The one who faced it glistened an
even brighter red. But not only from the fiery
glow; Cuin's heart turned over as he realized that
Bevan shone red with blood.

The priests of Pel yearned at the sight of it.
"Let us drink his blood, lord," they chanted huskily, "and feed his heart to the crows."

"He will yet be one of us," Pel intoned, and
ritualistically raised his gleaming knife. But Bevan threw back his head and laughed, a laugh
sweet as the fall of silver water.

"Will you yet be one of me?" he mocked, raising his hands and brandishing the thong that
failed to bind his wrists. "You know by now that
your blade does me small harm, O Mantled
Master. Put me in your pot, indeed, and give me
immortal life! For the son of Celonwy is not so
easily unhearted as yon poor shells of men."

"Hang his heart on the oak, lord!" the cloaked crowd roared.

"Come, mighty shadow!" Bevan coaxed. "Let us see you fail once more."

"Bring a spear," the hooded figure ordered harshly. Half a dozen cloaked servants scrambled to obey him. A bright lance was brought, and the mantled lord hefted it, testing its balance as he turned toward Bevan. . . .

Cuin sprang without plan of attack or hope of victory. The startled priests fell before him like grass, shouting the alarm. Through the hubbub Cuin sensed Bevan in swift motion, grappling with the mantled lord. . . . But Cuin could not reach him to aid him. The unmade men were all around him now, and he took cuts. The odds were hundreds against one; it would soon be over—

A cloud of sudden smoke darkened his sight, smoke so dense and stinging that it turned the combat into gasping confusion. Choking, Cuin felt a hand on his, and even in the smother he knew that warm touch. He and Bevan fled aimlessly into the darkness, and not until they were well beyond the walls did they pause for breath. Cuin hastily pulled off his shirt.

"Put this on," he whispered, "or you'll leave a bloodspoor. Here. . . ." He could feel Bevan trembling with pain as he helped him on with it.

"Where are the horses?" Bevan gasped.

"North," Cuin sighed. "But where is that? I cannot even see a star, in this hellhole. Can you tell, Bevan?"

"Nay. . . ." Bevan's voice told Cuin that he could hope for no more help from him that night.

He had forgotten Flessa. When her weight

touched his shoulder, he jumped as if he had been stabbed. Then he laughed shakily. He heard her flutter away to the left.

"Follow the falcon," he muttered, and plunged up the slope, half-dragging his comrade. When they reached the horses at last, he had to hoist Bevan onto his. Shouts arose faintly from the Pit far below. "Which way?" Cuin asked.

"North, to the Forest," Bevan managed to answer.

Cuin could see the constant star now. He attempted no subtlety on this flat southern land, but set a course straight as an arrow. The steeds were rested and willing to run. When dawn came, Cuin could see no pursuit for miles behind them. But what he saw beside him made him sick at heart. Bevan lay with his head on the horse's neck, and his face was as gray as the dawn.

When they came to a watering place, Cuin got him down and peeled off the shirt that was stiff and brown with dried blood. Shock like a sword thrust tore through him as he saw how Bevan was mutilated. This had been no idle torture; Pel had earnestly tried to kill him with stabs and slashing blows that should have slain him a dozen times. Shakily, Cuin tried to wash the wounds, but he knew he had no healer's skill. Sudden tears of helpless agony ran silently down his face and dropped onto the limp form beneath his hands. Bevan stirred, opened his eyes and gazed in wonder.

"Cuin," he whispered painfully, "I am abashed. I knew you were of mighty heart, but I would scarcely have thought that you could love me."

Cuin winced at the words, though love indeed was what he felt for this wayfaring stranger from

the hollow hills. "Save your strength," he said
roughly. "I must get you to a leech, somehow,
though I am sure those unhearted ghouls will be
hot after us."

"Nay, to the Forest, Cuin! Once I have lain in
the woven shade I will be well. The balm of my
mother's blessing flows in the beech and the silver
poplar. . . . Is it far, Cuin?"

"How should I know? But the horses travel
well. Come, let us be moving."

Cuin got Bevan wrapped up a bit and onto his
dapple-gray steed, and they were off again. They
kept a swift and steady pace through the day,
though Bevan clung to his horse's neck and Cuin
feared lest he fall. The land changed gradually to
gently rising ground, as wild and open as the
Downs but clad in shaggy brush. Cuin looked
about as they topped every rise; he was comforted to see no pursuit in the distance. And as
the sun dipped westward he was the more comforted to spy ripples of darker green before them.
The Forest was not far.

They reached the shelter of the trees by sunset,
and Cuin pushed on into the dusk, searching for
he scarcely knew what. At dark he found it: pale
trees encircling a whisper of water. The carved
shrine above the spring marked the sacred place.
Cuin laid Bevan in the thick bank of ferns beneath the largest tree. The moonlight rimmed the
surrounding grove in silver. Gracefully as maidens
the slender circle raised a woven crown to the
sky.

All night Bevan lay still in the fragrant ferns.
Cuin sat silently by without even a fire for comfort; Flessa perched as still and unsleeping in the
closest tree. The horses quietly cropped the grass.

Toward dawn the white hart appeared and lay down serenely near the spring. Only then did Cuin begin to hope, and the hope tore him worse than the despair.

CHAPTER TWO

Bevan did not stir for dawn or sunrise. But when full light had come, a gentle light in that place of shifting shade, he gave a muffled cry of surprise and sat up. Cuin went to him quickly.

"What is this?" asked Bevan, bewildered. "I do not remember coming here."

"You have been asleep," Cuin told him. "How do you feel?"

"How should I feel? Well."

"You may recall," Cuin said tartly, "that you have been sorely hurt."

"Ay, that I was, indeed!" Bevan winced, but his mind swerved willy-nilly to his new wonder. "So that is sleep!" he marveled. "It is very healing, but can men need such healing every night?"

"I have not slept these three nights past," Cuin scolded, "nor eaten in as many days, on your account!"

"Then eat!" Bevan pointed to where fruit and cakes sat on the shrine close at hand. "Why are you angry, Cuin?"

"Because you took a fool's path which might have been the end of us both, and because . . ."—Cuin sank back on the ground,

suddenly spent—". . . because I am a coward,
Bevan. I cannot admit even to myself how glad
I am to see you alive."

"You make a quaint coward," Bevan told him
softly, "who leapt singly against scores of foes for
my sake. Come, Cuin, eat and rest; put care from
you for a while. The others will watch."

"First let me look at you," Cuin said gruffly.

The wounds were dry and healing cleanly. Cuin
bandaged them carefully, then brought the food.
He sat beside Bevan to eat his share. Then he lay
down where he was and slept within the moment.
When he awoke, in late afternoon, Bevan lay beside him dreaming with open eyes as was his
wont. Cuin rose to find a neat pile of game at his
feet; Flessa had been been hunting. He went a bit
beyond the grove to make his cookfire. He felt
that it would not be right, somehow, to kindle
mundane flame within the sacred place. He
cleaned and spitted the meat for roasting. Presently Bevan joined him.

"Tell me what chanced," Cuin said. "When
were you captured?"

"Soon enough!" Bevan grimaced, mocking himself. "You were right to be vexed, Cuin. I thought
I had to go there, but it seems to me that I went
much overweening. I looked to find no evil in
darkness, but the fair black of the raven is not
the black of the crow. . . . Even the dark of the
moon is shining light to the gloom of that Pit. I
fairly lost my way. I had to make a light at last,
and then of course they had me at once. They
need no better guard than that shadow. It is a
substance and a weapon in itself. It frightened me
as shades of the dead frighten men; it chokes the
heart and bends the mind—"

"Then you were taken even before dawn," Cuin interrupted.

"Ay. They beat me, but nothing worse during the day. They prefer to do their bloody rites by night, it seems. Indeed, I did not see the mantled lord until after dark. He puzzled me, that one. I could see no face beneath the hood."

Cuin shuddered. "I thought I saw you run at him."

"Only because he came between me and the fire. I could make little of him. I felt cloth, and then he slipped from my grasp like a formless thing. Then I went to the vessel of youth. That is marvelously wrought, gold like blood of the sun and pearls like tears of the moon. . . . Coradel Orre it is called in the language of the elder folk: 'Caldron of Gold.' There is no evil in that basin, but it was withheld from serving me by a strong will, and I was in haste. The fire was amenable to my touch."

"The smoke served us well. But what could the caldron have done?"

"What Coradel Orre has given, it can take away," Bevan replied. "The unmade men who live by its doing could die by its withholding. And were it freed from its hooded master, then other men, mortal men the ever dying, might know it and live." Bevan's dark eyes were yearning.

Cuin stared. "It was for that you went!" he exclaimed.

"Ay. Could I have found my way to Coradel Orre and schooled it to my will, much sorrow and strife might have been saved, and much glory won. . . . But I have failed. And I warrant you I will not return to Blagden now a while."

"You might have told me what you were about,"
Cuin muttered.

"Ay, that I might." Bevan met his gaze candidly. "It is not only in enmity that I have failed,
Cuin. I have showed a weakling in friendship, as
well."

Cuin reddened. "Do not judge yourself so
harshly," he mumbled. "You know I hated you
once. But it is true, Bevan, that now I would serve
you in—in all love."

"As I would lead you in all troth," Bevan whispered, moved. "Shall we make it a pact, Cuin?"

"Pact," Cuin replied, and they touched hands
to seal it.

They stayed a few more days at the grove of
Celonwy. Cuin feared pursuit, but the news Bevan
heard was that Pel and his servants were keeping
to Blagden. It seemed that Pel was no more eager
to seek Bevan at this time than Bevan was to
seek him. The mantled lord had lost face in the
confrontation, for such a chieftain is ever as
much at the command of his warriors as they
are at his. Pel Blagden would strive for better
advantage before he came to grips with Bevan
again.

On the third day a little group of peasants
came to the shrine, bringing offerings. They scuttled off in a fright when they saw the strangers,
and once they had eaten, Bevan and Cuin thought
it best to leave. They went gently, for Bevan was
not yet strong. Though his wounds were healing
rapidly, he tired quickly. It would be well into the
autumn before he regained his former strength.

They traveled northward, toward Eburacon and
Myrdon and the Wildering Way. First they came
to the sluggish, dark river that watered these

southern lands, the river that some folk called
Pel's Moat. They followed it inland for a while.
Many lords dotted their holdings about these
parts, and some of these Bevan made shift to
meet.

Cuin could not help him here; he knew nothing of these folk. But Cuin noticed that Bevan
needed little help these days to make his presence
felt and remembered. He had changed somewhat
since Blagden; there was a harder set to his fine-
chiseled jaw, a harder sheen to his dark eyes. No
longer did he quarrel with the fate that had set
him against the mantled lord of Blagden. Now
his entire will was bent to the conflict: for revenge, for peace, and, indeed, for the defeat of
Death itself through the magical caldron. . . .
Only Bevan knew what his dreams were for
Coradel Orre. But his dreams directed his days,
and even his swordsmanship improved, though he
still wielded a battered and rusty blade.

By mid-September they had skirted Eburacon.
Even if Cuin had been able to pass the barrows,
neither of them desired to visit this place, where
every stone spoke silently of Ellid. . . . It became
evident that they were going to Caer Eitha, and
they argued, delicately, what their plans must be.
Cuin was for wintering at Caer Eitha or Wallyn.
But Bevan had heard that Pel's priests were traveling again.

"We dare not hold still for them," he said.
"Winter will not stop them. They are consummate servants to their faceless master, unhearted
things that they are; they will obey any command
without fear or compunction, and cold means
nothing to them."

"What would you do, then?" Cuin sighed.

"We will find friends where the road takes us, and with first spring we will summon them to our aid. By summer we should be ready to march on Blagden—if men can agree."

Cuin's brown eyes sparkled. "My uncle alone could raise a force sufficient for that."

"I do not doubt it," Bevan remarked mildly. "But if the High King is to keep the peace of this kingdom, it will take more than Pryce Dacaerin's say-so."

"I mean only that he can be of great help to you. And of course he has the Speaking Stone. You must needs make him party to your summoning."

"It will take more than the Stone, also," Bevan mumbled. The plan weighted him with reluctance, though he could not say why. Other problems burdened him, perplexities of mortality and longing and the lady that he and Cuin did not name. "Cuin," he said abruptly at last, "there is one who is ancient even in the memory of my mother's people, and full of wisdom. Let us go to her and see what she has to say to us."

"Where?" Cuin asked, startled.

"Not far. A few days hence."

It was a day's ride from the Wildering Way, and only two days' ride from Caer Eitha; it seemed odd to Cuin that he had never noted the place before. It was only a valley with a cottage and a little stream, a few chickens and a garden plot; but there was a strange radiance about it all. Inside the cottage sat the old woman working at a loom. She was ancient indeed, but there was no infirmity in her movements or her placid glance.

"Welcome, Bevan of Eburacon. Welcome, Cuin Kellarth," she greeted them.

Cuin glanced inquiringly, and Bevan gave him a rare smile. "It means Cuin of the Steadfast Heart."

"So he has been called since Time began," the old woman said matter-of-factly.

Bevan sank onto a stool by her side. "What is that web, Ylim?"

"I weave the threads of days and dreams," she said. "The days are troubled of late, but the dreams are good. Look."

Cuin came closer to see. The cloth glowed with colors that were more alive than dye could make them. It was midnight-blue for the most part, or so Cuin was to remember it, but it was also hues of moonlight and storm clouds, Pit-blackness and the gleam of distant armies. Through it all leaped the form of a great white hart crowned in silver; it seemed to move before the eyes. Cuin blinked; he thought he saw blood on the stag, but then all went to confusion for him. He turned away his head.

"What have you seen for us, Ylim?" Bevan asked.

"You should be the greatest of the High Kings," the old woman replied, "and Ellid Ciasifhon should be your Queen."

Bevan flinched and glanced sidelong at Cuin, who met his eyes with painful reassurance.

"But that is a dream, Bevan," Ylim continued gently, "and you know the pattern is ever changing. You do not need me to tell you these things. What troubles you, son of Byve?"

Bevan was silent; they all waited for his reply.

"Pryce Dacaerin," he burst out at last, to Cuin's surprise. "What of him?"

Ylim stared for long moments. "He has not yet resolved the bent of his mind," she said at last. "He is the father of your sweetheart, and for that reason alone he should cleave to you. But he is a proud and ambitious man, and the love of his child does not always constrain him. I believe you must strive to make him your friend, Bevan, but yet you do well to be wary of him."

"I have not known Pryce Dacaerin to do dishonor!" Cuin exclaimed.

"Nor have I," Bevan soothed him. "And in times to come, likely he shall set my worries all to naught."

"Declare yourself from Caer Eitha," the seeress told Bevan "and scruple not to call on the power of Pryce of the Strongholds and on the saying of the Stone." Ylim shifted her gaze. "But what thought is in you, son of Clarric?"

"That Bevan of Eburacon is much man," Cuin told her. "Deep and subtle are his own powers, and mighty is my uncle's power to aid him. But if he is to win his throne, he will need power to dazzle the eyes of men of shallow sight. Above all, it seems to me, he will need a kingly sword."

"You are well named, Cuin." The ancient seeress studied them both, gauging their strength. "There is such a sword to be had in Lyrdion," she said presently.

"I do not know that place," Bevan said.

"I have heard of it," Cuin remarked, "but I do not understand what happened there."

"That memory had faded in men when Byve was a boy," Ylim mused. "An age before the High Kings of Eburacon ruled Isle, the Royal House of

Lyrdion came to woe. But great was its power before pride overtook it, and great power yet resides
in its chiefest treasure: the sword. Hau Ferddas is
its name, 'Mighty Protector,' and he who wields it
cannot be vanquished by force. Yours is the birthright, Cuin, for you are of that lineage, through
your mother's folk."

Cuin gaped in astonishment. "Where now is
this sword?" Bevan asked.

"It lies in the treasure barrow at Lyrdion, along
the Western Sea. Dragons guard the place."

"Dragons I can deal with," Bevan sighed, "but
there is a destiny laid on me that I may not behold
the sea."

"I know it well, Bevan of Eburacon. Therefore,
behold it not! Cuin must get the sword for you."

"Is it to be Cuin's lot," Bevan asked ruefully,
"ever to give up his birthright for my sake?"

"I cannot answer that," Ylim replied, "unless
Cuin asks it for himself."

"I ask it not," said Cuin quietly.

"Great is your gift of love, Cuin Kellarth," the
seeress told him, "and great will be your pain in it.
May the Mothers comfort and guide you well."
But Cuin hung his head in unease at her words.

They ate with the ancient woman, and they
could never afterward remember what had been
that meal. Then they went on their way with the
enchantment of deep time upon them and the
threads of Ylim's web before their eyes. "Who is
she?" Cuin demanded at last. "She is no goddess
that I have ever heard of, Bevan. Is she one of the
Mothers?"

"Nay," he replied dreamily. "The ages wash
over her like tides. Before the Mothers brought
man to Isle there were the Gods, and before the

Gods there were the Old Ones, and before either there was Ylim. She is a part of none of it; she is here still, and no one does her reverence. She weaves."

"Then she is the master of us all," Cuin whispered.

"Is it the dancer or the piper who is master of the dance, or yet the one who made the tune? But Ylim is one who sits aside. She catches the dance in the web of her loom, but I think—she makes it not."

Bevan paused; his dark eyes had grown as deep as distant skies. It was moments before he spoke again.

"It may be that there is One in whose sight she is younger than the dawn."

CHAPTER THREE

Golden leaves were falling as the six souls journeyed to Caer Eitha. The silver-crowned hart shone among them as strangely as an otherworld thing, but Flessa flitted through them like a kindred being. Achingly, irresistibly, Cuin was drawn to think of Ellid, of her flashing spirit, her quick golden lightness. . . . In no wise had he ceased to love her. But his love for her and his love for Bevan had struck a perilous balance which eased him somewhat; pain of self was lost to its abeyance. Such was the quality of Cuin Kellarth that he could only seek to aid Ellid's happiness.

"Tell no one in Caer Eitha of Lyrdion," Bevan requested as they neared the gates.

Cuin nodded assent. It was the way of a wise man not to boast of a deed until it was done. And if Bevan had another reason, Cuin chose to ignore it for the present. Quietly, almost casually, they entered the stronghold that, by the reckoning of Cuin's people, was his birthright and his home.

Ellid saw them coming from her upper chamber; her heart leaped in consternation and delight. Pryce Dacaerin also saw them come; he was as surprised as Ellid but far less pleased. He had thought that Cuin was yet in Wallyn, for he had not sent for him and Clarric had given no word. That his nephew should have joined with the so-called son of Byve was a chance Dacaerin had not reckoned on, and it complicated his half-formed plans.

Nevertheless, the lord received Bevan and Cuin with warm courtesy, expertly masking his misgivings. He met them in his great hall with courtly formality.

"My greeting to you and the welcome of my land and people," he told them.

"Let fortune prosper you and yours, Pryce Dacaerin," Bevan replied equably. "How fare your wife and gentle daughter?"

"Let the ladies come to us," Pryce bade a servant.

Ellid had not been idle since Bevan had entered the gates. Indeed, she had put the whole women's quarter into a flutter of activity. But despite the tumult of her preparations, she came before the company with quiet grace. Bevan gazed on her, as staggered as Cuin had ever seen him.

Her tawny hair had grown and was smoothed back under a net of gold; delicate beads of gold showed at her throat and wrist. In her russet gown she was as soft and sleek and mobile as the quick creatures of the wilds. Although she made no gaudy show, yet she was dazzling to look on, and she knew it well. She went first to Bevan and smiled into his widened eyes.

"What, my lord," Ellid teased softly, "do you not know me with my hat on?"

Bevan stepped to her quickly and gave her the kiss of courtesy, perhaps a trifle too long for courtesy. Cuin barely touched her cheek with his lips, brother-like. Then he went to embrace his aunt, the round-faced Eitha, who stood looking on Bevan with mingled doubt and awe. Dacaerin's tender-hearted wife feared for her daughter's contentment, if Ellid should cleave to this warlock Prince. But Pryce watched with satisfaction; he judged now that he saw the path clear which would lead him to power over a kingdom of men.

They feasted that night, for Pryce Dacaerin wished to do honor to his royal guest. Bevan spent the next day closeted with his host, forming plans, and the evening he spent with Ellid. The following day he and Ellid went riding.

None of this was easy on Cuin. He found himself at loose ends, for his uncle seemed to have little to say to him; and of his own accord he kept far from Ellid. Once he wandered unawares into the room where she sat with Bevan. They were holding hands, and Cuin saw the tension that filled even that small embrace at his approach. He left as quickly as he decently could.

"What do you think of all this?" his Aunt Eitha asked him worriedly. He saw more of her these days than of anyone else, for she kindly strove to fill the gap the others had left in his time.

"Of Bevan? He is bold of deed and deep of wisdom. My cousin has chosen well in choosing him." Cuin smiled whimsically. "If she keeps herself from me, that is her faithfulness, Aunt. But can you tell me why my uncle turns away his eyes?"

"I daresay it is only because you are so changed." Eitha sought to excuse her husband, though she also was puzzled by Pryce's demeanor. "You are not much like the little boy we once knew! Go to

him, Cuin, and perhaps you can put it to rights
between you."

So Cuin went, but to no avail. Dacaerin received him coldly and gave no worthy answers to
Cuin's carefully voiced concerns. In fact, Eitha
had spoken more truly than she herself credited
her words. Cuin was no longer the stripling warrior who had followed Pryce Dacaerin with youthful adulation. These days his loyalties were quieter
and his steady brown eyes saw clearly and deep.
The past few months had seasoned Cuin more
than he himself knew. But Pryce Dacaerin perceived his new stature, and felt it mostly as a
threat.

Cuin passed the evening in halfhearted revelry
with old comrades among the soldiery. He went
early to his bed, but did not sleep. Sometime after
mid of night Bevan entered his chamber and
seemed to know at once that he was awake. "We
will leave on the morrow," he said.

"How so, Bevan?" Cuin sat up anxiously. "Can
you be at odds with Ellid already?"

"Nay, nay. It goes well." A soft vibrancy in
Bevan's voice told Cuin all that he cared to know
of how well it went indeed. "But we will go to-
morrow, nevertheless."

"We need not go on my account," Cuin protested. "I am content." The lie showed plain even
in the darkness; Bevan snorted at it.

"Can you be flesh and say that?" he retorted.
"We will go in the morning. Get some sleep."
Bevan pressed a hand briefly to Cuin's forehead.
Cuin noted how the hand shone silvery-pale in the
faint light from the window. He noted Flessa's
hunched shoulders where she sat drowsing on her
perch. Then peace came over him and he knew

no more. He did not even see Bevan leave the room.

Cuin slept soundly and arose late. It was nearly midday when he and Bevan left Caer Eitha, for farewells took some time. To Cuin's surprise, Ellid made no fuss at their departure; she saw Bevan off with a dignity that heightened rather than hid her love. But Pryce Dacaerin was angered that they flouted his hospitality.

"It is well for you, Prince, that you may roam where you will," he growled, "but my sister-son should stay here. His first duty lies with this domain, that will be his to govern someday."

"By my troth," Bevan replied evenly, "I would rather lose my right hand than lose Cuin's love and companionship. But as for duty, the decision must be his."

"I will return in the spring," Cuin told his uncle without heat.

"Say you so, indeed!" Dacaerin roared. "Now hear me, sirrah; the decision is *not* yours to make! By the law of our people, I have authority over you, and I bid you stay! Disobey me, and you risk the loss of all that is mine to give. Heed me well!"

"You have little to give that has not already been withheld," Cuin replied quietly. "Farewell, Uncle. Farewell, Cousin." He kissed Ellid quickly, the kiss of friendship, and vaulted onto his steed. Bevan already sat his dapple-gray; he leaned to embrace Ellid once more before they turned to the gates. Behind them Pryce Dacaerin stood choking on his wrath.

They journeyed northward. For an hour or so they traveled in silence. Like a shimmering shadow, the white hart joined them.

"You should have asked Ylim that question concerning birthrights," Bevan said heavily at last.

Cuin laughed ruefully. "I expect mine uncle will think better of his threat. He is like that; he rages about a trifle and then forgets it when he is cool."

"And if it is no trifle?" Bevan asked in a low voice. "And if he does not forget, but hardens to his word with time, as a proud lord will? What will you think then?"

"As I think now—that my first duty is to be a man. Be easy, Bevan; it was not you who made the quarrel." Cuin's smile faded into a frown. "Though you may be one who suffers by it! What if he withholds from you the Stone, and his support? Or even—Ellid?"

"Those things he shall not do." Bevan spoke with settled certainty. "He is ambitious on Ellid's account and therefore on mine. He will aid me to the top of his bent. But he fears any power that is not his own, and therefore he wishes to separate us, to keep you by him where he can put a rein on you."

Cuin stared incredulously. "You credit him with monstrous cunning! Yet you gave him fair enough speech."

"He is your kin, and Ellid's," Bevan replied quietly. "It is true I think him a schemer, but he is sire to such glory that I look for good from him yet."

At nightfall Bevan and Cuin stopped to eat, but not to camp. "We will go on a while in the dark," Bevan explained, "and then turn west toward Wallyn. There is no need for your uncle to know whither we travel."

"As you will," Cuin replied wearily. "We had a

late start, and the horses are rested. But I think
you are moonstruck, Bevan Celonwy's son!"

"Do you think so, in truth?" Bevan eyed him
quizzically. "Let me show you."

Leaving the horses and gear, he led Cuin afoot
back the way they had come. Following him
closely, Cuin moved as quietly as he could in the
dense shadows beneath the trees. After less than
a mile they came to a campfire. Cuin could scarcely believe what he saw. Around it dozed men he
had known from his youth; trackers he knew them
to be.

"So let us go," Bevan breathed in his ear.

They rode northward through the night. Toward dawn they chose a rocky stretch of soil to
turn sharply westward, and they rode westward
through the day. That night they rested, and after
a week without further incident they came to
Wallyn. Bevan judged that they had lost the
trackers. Not that it greatly mattered, for those
who trailed them wanted tidings, nothing more.
Still, in the properest spirit of Dacaerin's conniv-
ing, they rode into Wallyn by night. Clarric was
sorrowful to hear what had chanced at Caer Eitha,
but not surprised.

"I knew we were risking Dacaerin's displeasure
when I let you go a-roving," he remarked to Cuin.
"He is not one to lightly abide another loyalty.
You'll note I made no rush to tell him of your
whereabouts."

"I spoke him soft," Cuin mused, "but what he
wanted from me I could not give him. After facing
Pel's priests I could not tremble before him as I
used to. At his very worst, Pryce Dacaerin can
but slay me!" He laughed, and Clarric smiled
crookedly.

"I trust it shall not come to that! Ay, you've grown, lad, and I believe it is not only Pel's Pit that has changed you. . . . Well, I hope your uncle will think better of you in time. Shall you winter here?"

"Nay. By frost we hope to come to Lyrdion."

"Lyrdion!" Clarric seemed strangely shaken by that one simple word. "My lord Bevan, is this your behest?"

"It is at Ylim's advice that we go there," Bevan replied. "For myself, I know little of it. I would gladly hear your thought."

"Ylim!" Clarric's tone had subsided to one of quieter wonder. "That also is a name of fair peril to me. I have no thought to offer you, Bevan of Eburacon, only fear. Six months ago, or even less, I would have locked Cuin in chains sooner than let him venture to that place of ancient dread and grandeur. But now I have seen that he is a man, and I can only say to him: Beware! Lyrdion is a place of deepest danger to one of your mother's proud blood, Cuin. I charge you: remember always how long have been the years since your mother's Mothers were the begetters of Kings beside the Western Sea."

"So long the years," Cuin remarked, "that I have never heard of such Kings till lately."

"Even so."

"But it is not of warlike peril that you speak, Father."

"Such peril there may be," Clarric replied heavily, "but it was not of such that I spoke."

"Then tell us, my lord Clarric, that we might know," Bevan requested, "what has chanced at Lyrdion."

"Is it my place to tell you what the seeress did

not?" Clarric smiled faintly. "I have told you what I can, you two. For the rest, may the Mothers defend you! Come now, eat and sleep."

"I will eat gladly," said Bevan, "but you need have no bed prepared for me, my lord."

"Surely you're not going back to the Forest?" Cuin asked worriedly.

"Nay, I'll stay within the walls for this one night."

"Better tell the sentries, Father," Cuin suggested wryly, "lest they be startled into shooting him. He goes like a shadow in the dark."

Clarric did so. Later, when all was settled, he made his way to his son's room. Cuin was wearily pulling the shirt from his scarred shoulders.

"Does that warlock not sleep at all?" Clarric demanded.

"Never, unless he is sorely hurt." Cuin heavily tugged the thick wrappings from his legs.

"But what does he do by night?" Clarric exclaimed. "Bay to the moon?"

"He wanders," answered Cuin stiffly, "and he talks to the creatures and to tree-spirits and to all the moving spirits of air. He takes on knowledge from moonlight and shadows. Sometimes he sings. I have heard him across the reaches of the dark, and no bard could surpass that sound for loveliness." Cuin blew out the lamp and turned to his narrow window. Clarric joined him.

"So you have grown to love him well."

Cuin was silent, and Clarric waited as silently for his answer. The darkness beyond the window took form before their eyes, and presently they could pick out the line of the faintly starlit battlements. A figure moved on the stone, the slender form of no sentry. It came to the highest place and grew still against the luminous sky.

"Ay, I love him," Cuin replied quietly at last. "Whether more in awe or in pity, I can scarcely say. He has powers and wisdom which have made me rich in wonder. . . . But his strangeness sets him so apart, even from me. We are faithful comrades, but yet. . . . Look at him. Have you ever seen a lonelier mortal?"

For a moment they silently watched the distant dark figure sitting against the stars.

"Still he returns your regard," Clarric remarked.

"I scarcely know," Cuin murmured. "He favors me with fairest kindness; yet I scarcely know. I have not known his heart."

CHAPTER FOUR

Cuin and Bevan left Wallyn the next night, slipping out by cover of darkness as they had come. They were well provisioned, and carried blankets and extra clothing against the autumn chill. The trees were almost bare. Between their dark trunks the earth showed bleakly brown. It was an unfriendly time of year to be traveling, and a verily villainous time of year to be traveling north. Yet north they must go, and they hoped by this folly to foil the spies of the mantled lord, or of anyone who cared to spy.

They were a fortnight in journeying to Lyrdion, for there was no beaten track or even cow trail to ease the way. The land was high and hilly and wild as the day it was born; not even robbers seemed to dwell in these parts. On the last day of October Bevan and Cuin smelled salt in the air, and stopped lest Bevan draw too near to the forbidden sea.

Above the naked trees they could see crags ahead, rendered liquid in the changing light of the setting sun. A moment later the flushed peaks went dark, and deep shadows were flung across the land. Night came that was soft and dense

as a black cat's fur. It was the night of the autumn fires, when witches were driven from the
harvest. Cuin knew that every hilltop in Wallyn
far behind him blazed with bonfires. But there
were no folk to kindle fire in these lonely
parts. . . . What, then, were the eerie flickerings
that shone across the dark from the distant tors?

"Fire-drakes!" Bevan exclaimed—as far as Cuin
could tell, in delight.

They sat in the dark and watched the bright
breath of the dragons on the seaward heights,
like children watching lightning before the storm
comes too close. All that night they kept vigil together, counting the fiery puffs on the black surface of the dark; the blue-green flames and the
rosy pink, the purple and the lavender. . . . Of all
his adventures, Cuin was never to know a time so
fearful and beautiful, beauty of dragons and
beauty of Bevan's comradeship. He never remembered a moon or stars in that night. When dawn
came at last he stretched stiffened limbs and
gazed, but not a dragon could he see; only the
bony-hard rock of a fell brown crag in the daylight.

"They have gone within," Bevan said softly.
"They are the Old Ones, they and the mountain-
giants and the small twisted folk who first delved
the hollow hills. They are lovers of the narrow,
dark places of the earth and of the things they
find there. Sunlight brings no joy to them."

He and Cuin ate a little, but neither of them
had much desire for food. Then they rode slowly
toward the jutting peaks to the west. Presently
they came to their rocky shoulders; a high defile
ran between their barren heads, and beyond was
the pounding of the sea. There was nothing for it

but that Bevan should remain behind the line of the tors. Cuin prepared to go on alone.

"Dragons are cool-hearted folk and slow to rouse," Bevan instructed him. "But their sluggish hearts are yet set in bitter memory of what they have lost and in greediest grasp of what remains to them. Iron and steel were their undoing, the hot forged metals that are alien to them. Your sword will ward them off, but it will enrage them, also. You must judge nicely. Yet think more on that other peril your father charged you with."

"If I come to harm," Cuin told him in a low voice, "lay it not to your account, Bevan. It is for my own sake that I venture here."

"I know it; else I would not part from you so lightly. But I do not doubt that I shall see you in good time. I will wait here. Farewell."

They touched hands; then Cuin sent his steed up the steep slope. He stopped at the top, awe-struck. Beyond the tors the land took a stunning drop to the sea. Away to the right was the ruin of a towering fortress, looming crazily between the rocks and the surf. But the landscape all around it almost dwarfed its grotesqueness. Weird shapes of stone soared out of the water at every hand. On their flanks sported great white birds and silver sea-drakes and things even stranger: sylkies and nikkurs, the soulless riders and horses of the sea. Truly Lyrdion was a place doubly protected; for if it took a bold man to come at it from land, it would take a lunatic to approach it from sea-ward. Cuin shuddered and turned away his eyes, for the vast waters were a shape of engulfing terror to him even without their shadowy den-izens.

He sent his roan slowly down the long descent

to the gravelly shore. Ages past, it seemed, this
had been a stone-paved track. The going was hard
but not impossible. Once down, he rode along the
shingle toward the ancient hold of Lyrdion, keeping as far as he could from the tumbling surf. The
sea creatures paid him no heed; indeed, he could
scarcely see them now over the foaming water.
But landward Cuin noted movement from the in-
volutions of the jagged peaks down which he had
come. Even as he looked, a long, gleaming red-
gold form launched itself and circled the air
above him on fluted cape-like wings. Then with a
harsh and mournful cry it came to rest on the
topmost towers of Lyrdion. From the rocky crags
a strange croaking chorus went up and fell away
at once to a waiting silence. Cuin felt the stare
of many alien eyes.

I have been announced, he noted wryly, and
patted his frightened horse. In a moment he came
to the gaping entrance of the keep. Tethering the
roan firmly, and fervently hoping that the dragons
would let it be, he entered the dark and ruinous
hall.

Light filtered through the drafty crevices of the
walls, dimly falling on ancient metal. Cuin stared;
a heavy golden throne still stood on the dais, its
rich ornamentation now complicated by cobwebs.
Heavy cloth hangings screened it; mice squeaked
among the folds. Someone's fine bone-handled
dagger and fork lay on a rotted trencher table, as
if waiting for a dinner of dust. Lyrdion had not
fallen to storm or siege, that so much had been
left in its accustomed place, Cuin thought. Plague,
perhaps? There were strangely-wrought weapons
still hanging from spikes in the stones. But none

of these, Cuin was sure, was the sword which he
sought.

He thought of exploring the tower chambers
which echoed above him. But some instinct
turned him instead toward the catacombs beneath. The crumbling stone steps were dark, and
he went cautiously. Once below, he moved down
a central corridor which ran inland, into the stony
tors. High, tiny windows showed him chains and
devices of torture rusting in the dungeon cells
he passed. Cuin's hair prickled; eerily he felt the
presence of the ungentle folk who had once peopled these halls.

He passed doorway after doorway, half-fearful
of each, before he realized that the bloody red of
the stone dungeon floors was not a reflection from
his mind. A gleam of dull red lit up the passageway. The garnet glow came from somewhere
ahead, not from the grisly chambers on either
side. Step by slow step Cuin moved down the
passageway until he could see the source: two
slowly pulsing whorls of ruddy light, ebb and
flow, ebb and flow. . . . With an effort Cuin stilled
his own panting breath, calmed the racing of his
own pulse, until he could hear the heavy breathing of the dark hulk that was the dragon. The
blood-red vortices were its nostrils. Clutching his
sword, Cuin took a step closer.

A snorting roar shook the dungeons of Lyrdion
as the dragon lit up its cave with a bright, fiery
glow. It was huge, larger by far than the others
Cuin had seen; it coiled like an ancient puzzle-
knot into its hollow beenath the rocky roots of the
mountainous tors. Its scales were glittering red-
gold, and a red plumy crest bristled from its
high-flung head. Yet it could not match the glory

of its own nest. It lay upon gold and gems; the
whole stony chamber was filled with them.
Jeweled chains and brooches, myriad coins and
ornaments were piled halfway up the walls.
Golden drinking cups, caldrons and flagons tumbled out of the heap. Amidst all the sparkle stood
the sword which Cuin sought. Hau Ferddas con-
fronted him.

It was a splendid weapon, shining gold and
studded with jewels, massive enough to slay by
its own weight. Even through the blazing sparkle
of the dragon's gemmy lair, Cuin had felt his eyes
drawn first to the sword. Crosslike it stood, with
its point encircled by a kingly crown, between
the black sheen of the dragon's clawed feet. Cuin
moved his gaze slowly up the rippling red-gold
flanks to the angular head. Over the sword the
dragon stared back at him with unblinking yel-
low eyes. The crimson fire of its nostrils kept up
a constant surge like the sea, and its silent scru-
tiny was disconcertingly aloof. The hardness in
those topaz eyes was too remote to be called
hatred, too impersonal to be called enmity. The
dragon looked sullenly out of the distances of
another place and time. Cuin secretly felt for his
voice.

"O ancient guardian of this fearful place," he
told it, "I am a son of the Mothers of Lyrdion,
and I come for the sword which is my birthright."
He could hardly expect that it would comprehend;
he hoped only for such an understanding as one
hopes for with a mettlesome steed. But something more passed between them; Cuin felt it
at once. The dragon narrowed its glassy eyes,
and its long, crested neck stiffened to attention.

"O golden one," he tried again, "I am called Cuin, son of Rayna, who was born of Reagan, a daughter of the line of Lyrdion. I have come for Hau Ferddas." He gave the sword its name in the Elder Tongue.

The result took him utterly off guard. He had looked for resistance, but instead a flood of welcome engulfed him, a tide deep as the sea beyond the walls. Though neither he nor the dragon had moved, Cuin felt as if he had been set upon strong and friendly shoulders. He was a comrade, a kinsman, a savior, indeed; all that he saw was his for the asking. Let him take the golden crown and place it on his head! Let rich chains be looped on his neck and jeweled armbands bind his wrists! For he would restore the glory of the ancient line of Lyrdion; all of Isle would bow to his might! He would be a warrior-king, dressed in breastplate and golden greaves. To Cuin it seemed that the blood of a hundred bright-helmeted warriors surged into his veins. He felt their bloodthirst, their brazen valor, their gaudy magnificence. He felt the multitude of their shades all around him, soundlessly chanting, urging him to fulfill them in their desires. But Cuin was ever loath to do as he was bid, and his spine stiffened against the voiceless clamor.

"Nay!" he cried. "You do not understand! I take it not for myself, but for one far greater than I. The very son of the High Kings and of Celonwy daughter of Duv—"

Instantly the dungeon air grew tense with enmity. The soundless chanting took on a deeper pitch, and Cuin was swept up in a dark flood of hatred. The Crown was old in Lyrdion generations

before the High Kings reigned. Kill! Kill! the
upstart son of a latter-day weakling called Byve.
They who lived on in the form of the Ancient Ones
needed no traffic with the goddess who had reft
them of their domain. Kill! Kill! the son of Celonwy born of Duv! Onward, Cuin of Lyrdion!
The invisible warriors roared.

So compelling was their unheard song that for
a vivid moment Cuin felt the entirety of their
vision. Why could he not be King! Was his line
not the more ancient and valiant? And who was
this Bevan of Eburacon that he, Cuin of Lyrdion,
should suffer his ambition to go unpunished? Any
man who would not bow to his rule, let him beware his wrath! Bevan of Eburacon would learn
the force of a sword in the hands of Lyrdion! The
red dragon-glow was the haze of Bevan's blood
before his eyes. The chant of the disembodied warriors pounded to a paean of triumph in his head.
Crown him Cuin Conqueror! they cried. *Cuin the
Mighty One of Lyrdion! Let the jewels of the
realm adorn his brows! Bring on the Crown!*

Suddenly utter revulsion gripped Cuin, a self-
hatred that shook him to his roots. The sight of
the golden hoard sickened him. Raising his sword,
he strode blindly forward. The great guardian
dragon roared with rage and sent forth a spray of
fire. Still it slowly retreated before him as he
reached Hau Ferddas. He seized the mighty weapon and spurned the encircling crown with his
foot. The royal diadem of Lyrdion spun away from
Cuin's kick and clattered against the stone wall.

"Thus I value your royal bondage!" he shouted,
choking. "Golden ghouls! You are blood-blinded
and galled with greed. To think that I would kill

him, he who is the fairest—Hell-wights! I will
leave this den of—of firebrands!"

He ran out at once, stumbling in his near-panic
to be gone from the place. He found his roan horse
trembling where he had left it, and trembling in
like wise he cast himself upon it. Dragons lined
the cliffs, watching, splendid gold-shining pres-
ences to the number of a hundred or more. Cuin
could not think of them as beasts only; he saw
them as great gold-mailed warriors, their crested
helmets plumed with fire. Crouched to his horse's
neck, he spurred past them and made for the
steep path down which he had come.

He held the heavy jeweled sword of Lyrdion
clutched clumsily within his cloak, loathing it,
anguished at his own frailty. As quickly as he
dared, he urged his roan steed up over the tors.
He was frantic to see Bevan, irrationally frightened lest his momentary wickedness should have
somehow done him harm. As he descended the
slope, terror gripped him; Bevan was not where
he had left him. But in a moment the Prince came
running from between the rocks. Cuin stumbled
down from his steed and into his comrade's embrace. Tears of relief and remorse slid down
Cuin's face; he ducked his head to hide them. But
then he became aware that Bevan had been as
stricken as himself.

"By tides and tempests, Cuin!" he exclaimed
shakily. "I am glad to see you! I should never have
let you go. I have heard some talk since you left,
and you have been in such peril as I had not
dreamed. If you had taken any thing except the
sword from that dragon hoard, even so much as

a coin to remember it by, we would have met no more. You would have become—"

"One of them," Cuin murmured. "A dragon-lord."

"Even so. I am glad that you did not come to it. I need no sword from so cursed a place."

Cuin faced him whimsically, his composure somewhat regained. "Nay, I have your sword right enough," he remarked gently. "It is here." He drew it from under his cloak and offered it on opened hands. Bevan stared, first at the bright weapon and then at Cuin's tear-streaked face.

"This has been bought with pain I can scarcely understand," he whispered. "I cannot take it from you, Cuin."

"Take it, and fling it into Pel's Pit if you will!" Cuin's voice snapped, and new anguish leaped to his eyes. "I hate it! It harrows my heart. Bevan, take it quickly!"

Bevan reached for the sword with one hand and gripped it softly by the hilt, lifted it lightly upright and caressed the blade with tender fingertips. Cuin sank back upon the ground and gaped in amazement. Hau Ferddas gleamed as if lit from within. It seemed a weightless, skybound thing in Bevan's hand, and quick as a bird to his command. Its very gems took on warmth and life.

"I brought you a dead and deathly metal mass," Cuin breathed, "and with a touch you have turned it into a talisman of all good."

"Ay, for this is from Lyrdion but not of it, Cuin Kellarth. It is far ancienter than Lyrdion; maybe as old as Ylim, who told us of it. Look at the metal, the gold that glows red as if a heart pulsed blood within it! I believe it might be of the same stuff as Coradel Orre."

"It is your sword," said Cuin with profound conviction. "But how will you carry it?"

"Wrapped in a blanket. By the great wheel, I would use it on no smaller game than Pel himself. . . . Come, Cuin, it is but an hour or so till dark. Let us begone from this abode of firedrakes."

Cuin was quick to comply. But they had not ridden far when they came to a cairn of stones set among the Forest trees. Cuin vaulted down from his horse and found a good-sized pebble which he hurled onto the heap. Bevan glanced at him curiously. "Why did you do that?" he asked.

"It is the custom among my people," Cuin answered sheepishly, suddenly aware of his absurdity. "To ward off evil. Some dire deed has been done here."

"Ay, dire enough!" Bevan sighed. "I have gained some knowledge this day, Cuin. Perhaps you'll not like it, but I have said that I would have no secrets from you . . ."

"Say on," Cuin answered as they rode away.

"The King's name was Ruric, son of Celia of the line of Lyrdion. The sister-son was Cavan son of Ceru. . . . Ruric gloried mightily in his throne and his wealth, his warriors and his stalwart sons." Bevan turned on Cuin his raven-dark eyes. "With the help of some of the others he slew Cavan back there, beneath the trees."

"He slew his nephew and heir?" Cuin exclaimed.

"He slew his nephew and heir. Ceru and her people fled the place, and from her your mother takes descent. A year later her followers returned by stealth to raise the cairn, and they found

Lyrdion as you have seen. It is not known how the change took place. Folk say that the shade of a murderer must haunt the place of the deed, Cuin, but no shade received your stone today. Ruric still clings to his royal estate."

"Ruric still guards his gold," Cuin murmured, "together with his warriors and his stalwart sons. But who has said that they may not take the one who comes for the sword?"

"Who, indeed!" Bevan smote his thigh with his eager palm. "Cuin, you voice the question closest to my heart. Who governs the Old Ones and the Elder Folk of earth? Neither dragons nor shades of dragonish men bow to the Mothers or the Great Mother Duv. What constrains those who make their abode in Lyrdion?"

They rode on in silence; in silence the falcon flew to Cuin's shoulder and in silence the white hart paced by Bevan's side. Presently they reached a place of fire, and on a hilltop of that charred waste they turned to watch the sun set over the tors of Lyrdion. Blood-red light bathed the peaks. As they watched, a shape of winged brightness flashed between them and the sun. Soaring above the crags, the dragon circled, then breathed fire at the fiery sun and vanished. Even at a distance Cuin could not mistake that huge form.

"Ruric," he whispered. "The nephew-slayer. How my heart is torn, Bevan. Can you not feel it too, that he is magnificent?"

"If there is One who governs these things," Bevan replied slowly, "then it may be that such a One can bring beauty even out of evil."

They camped that night still in sight of the seaward tors. Cuin slept long, for a great exhaustion was on him, but Bevan wandered with the

silver-crowned stag. The next day they turned inland, and left Lyrdion's lonely demesne for a winter's hard journey through the barren northlands
of Isle.

BOOK THREE:
THE SUMMONING

Dark is the cloudy Pit, and dark
The mantled host that people it.
Bright is the new-sung King, and bright
The weapons that his legions bring.
Warriors shout and banners soar
When the White Hart goes to war.

Deep are the powers of Pel, and deep
The stony caves that form his hell.
High flies the golden sword, and high
The falcon o'er the wyvern-hoard.
Bold youth rides with ancient lore
When the White Hart goes to war.

Black is Blagden dell, and black
The evil that its slopes expel.
Argent is the Hand, and Argent
Shines the Crown of his demand.
Pel shall pay the long-kept score
When the White Hart goes to war.

CHAPTER ONE

In the fireside talk and the chieftains' Great Books, men were to call it the Winter of Bloodied Snow.

Nothing like it had been known in legend or living memory. In the freezing season when weather customarily kept the peace between even the bitterest enemies, in harshest winter, mantled bands struck like doomsters out of the comfortless Forest. The strange dark raiders seemed not to care for conquest, plunder, or the taking of women. Even though the surprise and terror of their onslaught often breached every defense of the small clan strongholds, still they would soon speed off again into the surrounding wilderness. But what they carried away with them seared the minds of the survivors. They took captives and the bodies of the dead; and of the latter they left behind the hearts.

Some few of the wiser folk, or those that listened best to the old tales of the siege of Eburacon, knew the meaning of the cloaked skirmishers and whither they took their grisly spoils. Fire glowed red in the depths of Pel's Pit, these deemed, and they tried to warn the others of the more horrible danger to come. But most were taken quite unprepared when the faces of former comrades glared out at them from beneath the shadowy hoods of the mantled raiders. Those who would not raise sword against them paid dearly; but those who saved themselves paid dearly too, for some went mad. It was not a thing lightly borne, to see a friend or brother fall and then to fell him yet a second time.

The southlands of Isle fared worst at the hands of Pel's priests, though scattered attacks were felt as far north as Wallyn. The far-flung domains of Pryce Dacaerin escaped much harm, for they were a hard month's journey to the north of the Pit. Pel Blagden's chiefest treasure constrained him to keep to his own terrain; Coradel Orre made clumsy luggage, but he was helpless to augment his armies without it. Through many generations of terror the mantled lord had never attempted conquest of Isle, for only the overthrow of peace-loving leaders was necessary. The unhindered avarice of the others was more than sufficient to engender the strife which fed Pel's rites and sated his appetites. Like the dark, flapping gore-crows, Pel's servants followed the scent of war. But there was no need for more bloodshed than the petty lords provided of their own accord.

Thus Pel Blagden had spread terror from time to time through many eras of men, and between times he had let terror be. And so short is the memory of man that only some few folk in Isle realized the meaning of the preparations of the mantled lord: that Bevan of Eburacon had set his will against Blagden, and that in the spring he would summon the chieftains of Isle to uphold him in his challenge. Great would be the gathering at Caer Eitha.

Through the long, dread-filled winter months Ellid sat at her window and sewed. She who had always been a restive needlewoman stitched diligently on bright-colored clothing to show Bevan royally in the eyes of the coming assembly. She feared for him with every fresh news of Pel's priests, and she prayed to the Mothers for his safe return. Yet, though she longed for him, in a sense Ellid did not miss Bevan; he had never been a part of her daily life. But more than she cared to admit, she missed Cuin.

She kept herself much aloof, even from the friendly groups around the great hall fires. More than once her mother came to her in concern.

"Why are you so much alone?" Eitha asked her one evening. "The lads and lasses wonder at you."

"My father has bade me keep my maidenhood of fair repute," Ellid replied bitterly.

Eitha sighed. Her husband had become harsh of late, almost a jailer to his wife and daughter. For the sake of peace Eitha bore Dacaerin's temper silently, but with her daughter she did not hesitate to speak her mind.

"There is no harm in honest companionship," she said huffily. "What ails you, lass? Surely your black-haired Prince would not take it ill if you drew nearer the fire!"

"Nay, no whit!" Eitha was still suspicious of Bevan, and to divert her Ellid spoke more of her true thoughts than she had intended. "I am worried about Cuin, Mother. Why is Father so enraged with him?"

Eitha sighed again and had no answer to offer. Silently she went away. Ellid sat and sewed; then she pricked her finger and wept. Cuin, her cousin and lifelong friend. When again might she hear his husky voice or sense behind his silence his constant regard? He, too, was in peril, but even if he lived and came again to her, she could offer him small comfort. Father and lover had severed her from him.

The thaw came, and Pryce Dacaerin sent out many messengers, as he and Bevan had arranged. Then true spring came at last. Soon visitors began to arrive. Clarric of Wallyn was among the first, seeking news of his son. Dacaerin gave him a cold welcome and colder comfort, but he answered mildly and settled in serenely to await the tide of time. Others rode in daily: petty lords and clan chieftains from all along the Wildering Way as far south as the Downs; from the western wooded hills toward Welas and from eastward as far as the Waste; from along the white-flecked Rushing River and the dark river to the south called Pel's Moat.

Most of these Pryce Dacaerin expected, but some he did not. There came a King of the barbaric tribes that roamed the far Northern Barrens; he and his retinue were fierce black-braided men whose broad chests jingled with jewels. Bevan, he said in his sonorous dialect, had healed his little daughter by the power of his comely hand. Also, there came an emissary of the Firthola, the strange fair folk of the bleak northeast who ventured upon the chilly Deep in boats. And the King of the ancient wanderers of Romany rode in on a sturdy pony of their special breed, ending his long journey from the eastern Waste.

At last in rode Cuin and Bevan, with weathered gear and a bulky bundle and the gleam of purpose in their eyes. Daring her father's wrath, Ellid ran out to meet them both.

"The Mothers smile on me!" she exclaimed, laughing, grasping their hands. "For many long days I have watched for you two, and today my patience is rewarded!"

Bevan regarded her with a rare smile, gazing at the golden lights in her eyes. "All such good ever come to you, Cousin," Cuin told her cheerfully. "And how does mine uncle?"

"Ill," replied Ellid sourly. "But here comes one who loves you better." Clarric came forward and hugged Cuin hard, kissing him. Then he herded him into the keep, leaving Ellid still holding Bevan's hand.

"You have grown yet again," Clarric said gravely, looking at his son. "There is restraint in your bearing and knowledge in your eyes. What did you find at Lyrdion, Cuin?"

"Much to fear and some little to love," Cuin replied, "and a goodly dose of humility, Father! I will tell you someday, but the time rolls upon us too fast now for tales. What have you heard here?'"

Clarric rolled his eyes. "Plots thick as porridge. Come, I will tell you." They went to his chamber to talk. In a darker chamber, not far away, Bevan kissed Ellid's eyes.

"There is some talk afoot of making mine uncle King in your stead," Cuin told Bevan late that night, after Ellid had gone to her bed. "Among his stewards, in particular, such feeling is strong. And many of the southern lords serve him well."

"That is just," Bevan replied. "Pryce Dacaerin is a valorous man. What does he think of this talk?"

"I cannot say. I have saluted him, but he only glares at me. As far as I know, he has said nothing to encourage or deny. His mind is a mystery even to my father."

"He will stay his word until he sees how the tide turns," Bevan decided. "He stands much to gain either way. . . . We can but meet them head on as we have planned, Cuin."

"Even so. But do not forget that there are those who are reluctant to battle against the mantled lord. Some even say that you are to blame for arousing his wrath."

Bevan grimaced wryly. "If only we could frighten him away with fire, like the demons of air!" he remarked bitterly, then left abruptly for his midnight wanderings. Cuin sighed and went to lie in his wakeful bed.

The next day the Summoning began in earnest. An odd assortment of men clustered around the great hall hearths and lounged against its rough-hewn pillars. On the dais, under close guard, was the cloth-draped form of the pedestaled Stone of Destiny.

Some fifteen kinds of priest were present, priests of Duv and of Bel and of many of the children of the gods; even priests of the wise and chaste goddess Celonwy. These all vied with each other to sanctify the proceedings, and their chanting went on for more than an hour. Presently Pryce Dacaerin ordered that the Stone be uncovered for them. They laid hands on it importantly, but none laid hands on it for long.

Then Bevan came forward. Ellid had made him a pearly white tunic of fine linen; it flashed on him like swordlight, but no more than the flashing of his thunder-dark eyes. Priests and onlookers alike froze to silence.

"Enough!" Bevan told the priests in a low voice that was heard by all. "My people loathe your empty words. Get you hence." They scurried to their places, and Bevan was left alone on the dais beside the Stone, surveying the assembly of those that by right were his subjects. "Are there those among you who would try the Speaking Stone?" he demanded.

Men shuffled their feet and glanced sidelong at their neighbors. But then Kael of the northern tribes strode forward, flinging his shining braids over his shoulders. "I am a King," he said. "I will try." He seized at the Stone, then shouted and jumped away.

"It burns!" he cried. Some men laughed, but Bevan faced him soberly. "You are my good and honest friend, my lord. Chance another will bear you out."

"It stings, right enough," Clarric spoke up mildly, "for I have had a look at it before. It may be that there is not a man in this great hall who could long lay hands on it." His words were like a goad, though gently spoken, and many came forward to prove him wrong. But none could bear the pang even for a space of a breath.

"Let our host of Dacaerin try!" one of the southern lords shouted at last, but Pryce shook his head in a way that suffered no argument. "Another of that illustrious line, then. Cuin? Where is the sister-son?"

"Here," replied Cuin from his place by the wall,

and he vaulted to the dais to let his words be
heard. "But I take no part in this quaint game. It
would be traitorous in me even to think it, knowing what I know and seeing what I have seen. There
is one before you, men of Isle, who stands your
King in birth and in deed. Let the son of Byve make
proof of his greatness!"

All eyes were fixed on Bevan where he stood
like a shimmering white flame in that dim place.
Lightly he extended his shining hands and laid
them on the Stone. The deep voice that then
spoke sounded through the great hall, and many
men trembled with the strangeness of it.

"Hail to thee, High King of Isle!" the Stone
saluted him. "Hail to thee, heir of Byve and of
Veril and the mighty sons of the Mothers!"

Bevan stood peacefully as snowlight with his
hands on the Stone.

"Beware of treachery, son of Byve!" it told
him. "Forget not thyself in love of man or maid,
but think most of thy duty to thine inheritance.
Look always to strengthen Isle now and for gen-
rations against the evil from the east. The bless-
ings of all the people of Duv be with thee. Thrice
hail to thee, High King of Isle!"

Silence fell; the light faded from Bevan's hands
and he stepped back from the Stone. The gathering sat as if stunned. Only Cuin seemed unsur-
prised.

"Behold your King," he said quietly, "who in
every wise deserves your fealty, you who are
leaderless."

A hubbub of talk sprang up at this, and a big,
slow-seeming lord from the southlands near Pel's
Moat rose to speak the commonest thought. "Leaderless we may be, and feeling the lash of Pel's

scourge," said he, "but who is this young warlock, that we should look to him? No matter what his parentage, he deserves no better fealty than the force of his right arm can win him."

"Surely you have heard of his fame at the battle of Myrdon," someone replied.

"Ay; to face a dragon is valor; I do not deny it. But did he draw a sword there? I think the mantled lord would not turn as tamely as the dragon."

"Hear me a moment, my lords." Mild-mannered Clarric ascended the dais, and even the most quarrelsome lords grew silent and hearkened to him men named Wise.

"Consider, chieftains of Isle. I have a son, a valiant young warrior, heir to Pryce Dacaerin"—Clarric coolly met Dacaerin's hard gaze—"and he cleaves to this son of Byve like a lymer for faithfulness. That alone should tell you something, though my lord Bevan is not one to boast, it seems. . . . But Cuin has told me that eight of Pel's priests who tormented my son at the oak were slain by the power of Bevan's sword. Moreover, Bevan and Cuin have been to Pel's Pit, even to the place of fires, and have returned alive to the upper air."

Talk buzzed again. "Is that true, my lord Cuin?" one of Dacaerin's stewards demanded. "That Bevan of Eburacon saved you from the servants of the mantled lord?"

"See the proof," Cuin replied, and slipped off his tunic. Even hardened fighters gaped at the marks of torture on his young form. Bevan winced and moved from where he had stood silent all this time.

"Speak further truth, Cuin," he remonstrated, "and say that they treated me even thus in Blagden, and that you leaped against a multitude to aid me." But Cuin's reply was lost in the gasp that went up all around.

"Say you so?" the steward shouted above the din. "Then is your case lost, lord! We can have no blemished King!"

"That is a saying of small men who would be easily rid of their liege." Bevan's melodious voice, though not raised, sounded through all the others; the great hall fell to silence at his words. "Who among us is not blemished in some way, my lords? But nevertheless, you shall have satisfaction. The son of Celonwy is not so easily marred." Bevan pulled off his pearly white shirt, and Cuin sank to his seat in amazement; on Bevan's graceful body the skin was as smooth as if it had never known sorrow.

"I wrapped you up! You ran red with blood!" Cuin whispered.

"Pel Blagden bloodied me, indeed," Bevan smiled at him, "but it was the Great Mother Duv who had the healing of me. Listen, you men of Isle!" Bevan rounded suddenly on the assembly. "For how many more ages of strife will you let the mantled terror stalk among you? Pel Blagden is a god, it is true, but he has spurned his right to reverence, and even an immortal can be slain. All that is needed is that you should stand together against him. Lend me but the numbers to hold off those heartless minions of his, and I will challenge him myself."

They all stared at him wide-eyed, but no man laughed; such was the force of his straight, slender presence. "How can you say that?" a southland lord asked at last, though not harshly.

"You who look not to be a warrior? Who do not even carry a sword?"

"I also am a son of the immortals," Bevan replied, "and I have weapons you know little of." He lifted his fair-formed hands. White flames rose from his fingertips, bathing the dim hall in achingly bright light; men winced in wonder. "Yet though they are sword-bright of themselves, my hands are not swordless," Bevan continued with quiet intensity. "A mighty sword has come to me, a brand far ancienter in power than even our ancient adversary." He flicked the light from his hands and reached through the sudden shadows to the bundle Cuin tendered him.

"Hau Ferddas!" Bevan cried, holding it aloft. The sword shone bright as his argent hand, but in color red-gold as the upward-striving sun. In its blood-red glow no one noted the flush of angry chagrin that surged to Pryce Dacaerin's face.

"Hau Ferddas," Bevan repeated more softly. "The Mighty Protector; the Peace-Friend which renders the wielder invincible in battle. Look on it well, men of Isle." And indeed all men stared for long moments, at the sword and at the raven-haired youth who held it. Great smooth gems gleamed on the weapon's hilt, and above them the golden blade soared like a tower above a rock, high and massive. Yet Bevan held it easily.

"The glory of Lyrdion comes to the heir of Eburacon," Bevan told the assembly, "in gift freely given by Cuin of that line. It must bode well, that the son of royal sisters should cleave to the son of a King of men. Old ways and new ways, clans and chieftains and lords of strongholds need not be ever at odds, it seems. But before there can be peace in Isle, we must rid our-

selves of that cloaked gore-crow who casts his
shadow to the south! And I tell you once more,
men of Isle, that with sufficient force to drive
him from his gloomy den I will beard him myself!" Bevan's gaze, like the flicker of fiery, dark
coals, held all men rapt in the glow of his flame-
bright sword. "Who will come with me to Blagden?" he challenged them.

"I will," Kael of the north replied promptly,
"though I stand little to gain and all to lose there-
by."

"And I," Clarric added quietly.

"And I pledge myself and my people," the
weathered King of Romany spoke for the first
time. "Wars for land and crowns mean nothing
to us, but there is the turning of an age at stake
here. The great wheel moves, and choice is giv-
en to us, how we would spend the years after
the reign of the Mothers gives way to the reign
of the sons of men. . . . What ails you south-
landers? You stand the most to gain."

"The gypsy speaks truly." A tall southern lord
rose stiffly to his feet. "Moreover, we stand the
least to lose; already we are brought to our knees.
I would not be mean of spirit, to cling basely to
what small power remains to me. I will throw in
my lot with Bevan of Eburacon."

"I had a brother once," a voice spoke bitterly.
"Sweet will be my vengeance on his account,
whatever the risk. A craven could do no less."

"Let no one name me craven or strait-hearted,
long to suffer this tyranny of Pel!" another
shouted. "My men and swords go with the son of
Byve!"

The tide was started then. Within moments the
great hall rang with cheers as each lord stood

and shouted his pledge of support. Bevan did not fail to note that Pryce Dacaerin kept his silence until many others had broken theirs. But Cuin had no such consideration; his eyes shone with joy.

"Behold your King!" he shouted at last, and others took up the cry. "Hail, Bevan High King! A crown!" They turned to their host. "Among your many treasures, Pryce Dacaerin, surely there is a crown for him?"

"My crown awaits me." Men fell silent, hearkening to Bevan's words. "The Argent Crown of Eburacon awaits me at Blagden, where the mantled lord bore it after the sack of my fair city. Once I have regained it, then I will call myself King. You who have given me your word: I ask you for no oath of fealty until that day. For now you must be bound to me by your own goodliness."

"Greed, glory or goodliness; whatever binds us will serve," Pryce Dacaerin growled. "When do we march?"

"After planting. But let the kerns stay home; I will drive no quailing peasants to Blagden. Let only men of valor dare this task, the most trusted warriors of your retinues."

"Even so," the chieftains agreed, and whatever their goodliness, a faint light of hope dawned in all their eyes.

After the assembly had gone chattering to courtyards and chambers, Bevan came to Ellid. Sitting beside her he soberly told her all that had passed.

"So that if I live," he finished, "it seems you will be a Queen, sweet lady."

"Then have I all to gain and all to lose," Ellid replied worriedly, "and the crown is the least of it. But it comforts me that Cuin will go with you."

"Well it might! He is the second marvel of my life, that one. You had some small cause to love me, Ellid, but he had greatest cause to hate me, and yet he cleaves to me. His is a heart generous as the sun. Small wonder you cherish his friendship."

Ellid flushed and hung her head. "It was not my thought to be unfaithful to you," she muttered.

"Nay, I did not say that at all!" Bevan hastened to reassure her. "You are much like him, Ellid; I cannot doubt that you will be as steadfast to me as he. Thus am I doubly blest."

They kissed then, and it was a while before they spoke again. "Have you asked my father?" Ellid murmured at last.

"Nay. With his silence he gives his consent, I dare say, but yet I have feared to risk his spleen . . . What do you make of him, Ellid?"

"He is grown a stranger to me," Ellid replied heavily. "Of course, he was ever one to keep his own counsel—but it seems to me that my mother is saddened of late, though she says no word of complaint. The matter of Cuin must grieve her, but perhaps it is more than that. . . . If you wait for my father to mellow, Bevan, you will wait long. Since last summer I have scarcely seen his smile."

"I will go now," Bevan said, and kissed her, and left. He found Pryce Dacaerin alone in his counting room, scowling over his gold. In a few courteous words Bevan requested Ellid's hand to be his wife, and curtly Dacaerin gave his consent. There was more to be said, plans to be laid, strategy prepared. They did not speak of Cuin. When Bevan left he could not fault the answers he had received; but like Ellid he had received no fatherly smile.

CHAPTER TWO

Within a day most of the lords and chieftains
had scattered toward their homes, for it strained
the resources of even Pryce Dacaerin to feed so
many for long. Within two days Bevan and
Cuin also took to the wilds again, riding southward with Kael and his retinue. The Firtholan
and the King of Romany had sped toward their
holdings in the east, but Kael could not hope
to reach his tribes in the far north in time to
send a force to Blagden. Moreover, the dozen retainers who accompanied him were as worthy as
a hundred lesser men.

And within the month such picked bands of
warriors could be seen marching on every track
in Isle. In glittering gold armbands and broad
gold belts they came; their spears and bucklers
shone like silver. Eagerly their sandaled feet
plied the Forest ways. Bevan's challenge and his
legendary sword had fired his vassals with a cru-
sading fervor such as they had never known. The
tale spread quickly, and throughout the realm
youthful candidates vied to be allowed to accom-
pany their lords to Pel's Pit. Some looked for glory

and others for revenge, but every mortal who marched to that battle did so willingly.

In the warm days of early June, Bevan and Cuin came to the broad plains north and west of Blagden. There they stopped to gather force and lay their final plans. Soon Clarric joined them with a small troop and with his own sister-son and heir, an ardent youth scarcely fifteen years of age. And the lords of the dark river and the western hills came with the finest fighters of their demesnes. Enemy camped by enemy, and yet the word of black-haired Bevan constrained them to keep their peace.

Pryce Dacaerin came at last with a troop of nearly two hundred men drawn from all his holdings. Ellid and Eitha accompanied him in a closely guarded horse-litter; many men looked askance at the red-haired lord, wondering why he had brought his women to war. Ellid gave Bevan a banner in the device of a silver-crowned stag, white on a field of midnight-blue. He raised it over the camp, and men wondered at it, also, for few of them had seen the white hart.

Good guard was kept day and night, for the Pit yawned only a few miles away. But Pel kept to his demesne, waiting, it seemed, and spies sent at twilight could see nothing to report. By the time of the full moon all of Bevan's forces had gathered, except for the Firtholas from the great cove far to the north. So early on a bright morning of mid-June he ranged them into line of war and prepared to attack.

Though Bevan lacked no strength of command, he knew little of the strategies of warfare. He relied much on Kael and on Cuin to advise him, but necessarily Pryce Dacaerin had entered into their counsels. That morning it was Pryce Dacaerin who rode the lines, and Cuin went with him on Bevan's account, though he and his uncle scarcely spoke. Silently they came to the place where Ellid and Eitha stood by their bodyguard and their heavily curtained horse-litter.

"Have you said your farewells?" Pryce asked Ellid mockingly. Ellid flushed angrily but gave no reply. Cuin knew that she had; Bevan had gone this way not long before. He believed that Pryce knew it as well as himself. Ellid held her head high, but there was anguish behind the mask of her face. Cuin caught her eye and gifted her with a quick smile. But Pryce Dacaerin noted the look.

"Sister-son," he said abruptly, "we have had discord of late, but there is a thing I know you will not refuse me. Go with these women and guard them. There is no one I trust for the task as well as you."

For a moment the words seemed fair. But then Cuin felt the shock of Ellid's glance and knew that he must serve her better.

"My aunt and my lady are well guarded by trusty men," he replied quietly. "My place is by my lord."

"But I have bade you go from me!" Dacaerin faced him with perilous patience, as if correcting a balky child. "Obey me in this, Cuin, and you may yet hope for my reward."

"Nay, Uncle," Cuin told him gently. "I spoke of my liege lord, Prince Bevan."

Dacaerin went scarlet with angry mortification. For a moment he glared at Cuin speechlessly; then he turned on the guard. "Take these sluts well to the westward," he grated. "And you, sirrah Cuin, keep from my presence!" He galloped furiously away without another word. Eitha stared after him sorrowfully.

"Thank you, Cuin," Ellid whispered.

"Fear not so much for Bevan," Cuin remonstrated. "He is mighty, though his might is not might of arms, and the blessing of the Otherworld is on him."

"I know it," Ellid replied. "Yet will you stay by him?"

"I go to him now. Farewell, Aunt; farewell, Cousin." He embraced them both and went with Ellid's brief kiss burning on his lips.

An hour later he sat his horse and looked into the depths of Pel's Pit. Bevan was beside him, and a thousand high-mettled warriors stood ranged at their backs. At the gates and on the crooked road nothing stirred; on the deep and distant battlements nothing. In the courtyard close to the keep the mighty oak brooded in solitude. Its leaves were as shadowy as a thousand dark, concealing cloaks. But no minion of the mantled lord was in sight except the gore-crows flapping and cawing above, waiting for food of battle.

"It is a strange chance," Cuin remarked, "if Pel waits to be taken like a knave in a closet."

"I doubt not he has many a surprise in store for us," Bevan replied wryly. "Where in torment is Dacaerin?" His eyes searched the long rim of the Pit for the tall figure of the red-headed lord.

"Duv knows," Cuin answered wearily. "He is as furious as a singed stallion. He wanted me to go with the women."

"So he was trying to part us again." Bevan

glanced quizzically. "What may be his game, I wonder? —There he is."

Dacaerin stood at the fore of his men on the opposite rim, and the emblem of the red dragon fluttered over his head. Cuin and Bevan met each other's eyes; it was time. Eerily silent, the Pit gaped below.

"At the very worst," Cuin said shakily, "it will make a fine song."

"May the Mothers grant us life to hear it," Bevan muttered.

All that they would have said of love and thanks was unlucky to be spoken. So they only clasped hands; then Bevan lifted the great golden sword. Its gems flashed like fire, and like such a fiery gem Flessa soared from Cuin's shoulder and circled above. The trumpet sounded; the banner of the white hart floated high. From all sides bright-helmed warriors moved on the Pit as Cuin and Bevan sent their horses down the treacherous road.

While the foot-folk were still struggling on the barren slopes, a black cloud of Pel's making billowed up to meet them. In a moment it might as well have been night. The creeping substance of gloom all but obscured the bright daylight, and its thickness dragged on motion like a clutching grasp. But it was its strangeness that chilled men's hearts and stopped them where they stood. Then the cloaked riders rushed like substance of silent terror out of the shadow.

Strong warriors quailed and forgot their swords. But a shape of wonder spurred to meet the enemy. Bevan blazed with white light that burned a vault in the gloom, and Hau Ferddas in his hand shone fiery bright. Quicker than flight it moved, seeming of itself to leap to each hooded throat; even Cuin's skilled thrusts by Bevan's side could not match it. Pryce Dacaerin, not to be so out-done, forged afoot to the fray. The warriors shouted and hurled their spears as a dark tide of cloaked figures engulfed the vanguard and surged up the slopes to meet them.

Bevan's warriors faced plentiful foes afoot and on horseback. Yet they soon found that the steep walls of the Pit gave them an advantage of height and force. Many fell, but the rest cheered as they pressed forward. They fought to behead, as they had been told to do. At their fore the dazzle of the black-haired Prince lighted their way. Close behind him followed the banner of the white hart.

Presently the ground leveled and dim shapes of battlements could be discerned in the settled darkness. Kael's dozen black-braided warriors mounted captured steeds and slashed their way to Bevan's side. Cuin paused for breath.

"How goes it?" he asked Bevan obliquely.

Bevan grimaced at the query. "Well enough," he replied. "But this is only our first taste of Pel's power."

"How in suffering are we to take those walls?" Pryce Dacaerin grumbled.

"If there is no spell in the stone, they will yield to my touch." Bevan straightened on his dapple-gray steed. "Trumpeter, ho!"

The fellow blew the rally and the attack. Kael's retinue formed a wedge to help Bevan force his way to the walls. Others joined them; Pryce Da-caerin and Cuin fought mightily. Bevan wielded Hau Ferddas with more than manly might. But the going was hard. Bevan's warriors numbered

many more than the cloaked denizens of Blagden, but their longer encircling line gave them
only equal advantage on the level ground. Then
the van faltered as the emblem of the white hart
tumbled to the ground. Someone lifted it high
again. Glancing, Cuin saw that it was Clarric
who held the staff. Dene, the young sister-son,
strode by his side.

"Let the lad carry it, Father!" Cuin shouted.

"Even the lad thrusts a sword better than I!"
Clarric shouted back, grinning. "Let the fighters
fight; I will carry this stick!" The battle forced
them apart then, and Cuin could look for him
no more. More fiercely on his behalf he sent his
blade against the priests of Pel.

Duv's curse on the unmade men! Cool, pas-
sionless and unspeaking, they were harder than
serpents to kill; their bloodless tenacity chilled
the heart. But at long last the van came under
the deeper shadow of the wall. As Cuin and Kael's
men held off the enemy, Bevan laid his shimmering hands upon the stone. Nothing happened,
and he frowned.

"It is strongly wrought with the words of the
ancient art," he muttered. "But the gates can
only be worse. By fair Celonwy's love—" Suddenly Bevan's white glow vanished. Utter gloom
filled the Pit, and many men froze in despair; even
Cuin was taken aback. But instantly a rumble
and a splitting clamor of stone sounded through
the darkness. Then Bevan sat his horse once
again ablaze with fiery light. The shattered wall
lay heaped before him. The priests of Pel scurried away over it, disappearing like bats into
the shadows. The warriors cheered and crowded
after them.

"Keep your lines!" Bevan shouted.

He leaped his steed over the rubble with Cuin at his side. Kael and his retainers joined them; ten was their number now. They rode at the slow trot into the darkness, hearkening intently. A soft hissing sound arose about them. Bevan lifted his sword to its fullest height. Golden light flared from the tip, brighter than any fire; all the courtyard showed plain in its gleam. House-tall squatting shapes loomed between the riders and the keep. At the sudden light they woofed and sprang back on bulky haunches, snatching at the air with their dangling claws. Pinpoints of sultry light flickered from their nostrils.

"Wyverns!" Bevan exclaimed.

Startled cries arose from the ranks of the warriors. Hau Ferddas sank and spent its light, and every man stopped where he stood.

"Thellen na illant arle," Bevan called into the gloom, *"brangre trist tha shalde on gurn mendit!"* ["Dwellers of inmost earth, beware lest you serve an evil master!"] But even as the words hung on the darkened air, he heard shouts and the thudding of swords as the leaping dragons attacked his men. Bevan and Cuin spurred toward the sounds. The wyverns hastened away from Bevan's white-hot presence and shining sword, but behind his back more sounds of combat arose. Bevan muttered between clenched teeth.

"They heed me not, and yet they will not face me!"

The warriors fought from the protection of the ruined wall. A dull red glow marked the gaping mouths of their foes, and already two wyverns lay dead. "Come, Cuin," Bevan panted, and swerved his steed toward the remembered sight of the keep. In darkness they two alone sped toward it; only a glimmer of silvery light lingered on Bevan's hands. In breathless darkness and silence they came to the walls of the squat tower that sat like a plug in the twisted funnel of the pit. Bevan laid hands on the stone, then spurred his horse to the gates. Strain tautened his pale face as he touched the aged wood and iron. Tramping feet sounded from behind the bars.

"Come," Bevan whispered, and turning away they galloped back to the others. "I could not have done more had I stayed a fortnight," Bevan panted as they rode. "There is a power in that place ancienter than Ylim—here they come again."

Pel's priests were issuing from the gates, marching to join ranks with the dragons. "Surely it is time we were going," Bevan remarked to Kael when they found him battering a wyvern. "See to it that all who must be left are beheaded, friend and foe alike. . . . Trumpeter!"

Then sounded the notes of the retreat, and men started gently back toward the slopes. Cuin and Kael rode the lines to see that Bevan's orders were obeyed. The dead and badly wounded were beheaded so that Pel could not make them things of his unhearted service. Many men would have balked at this command but that they had seen the foe and knew the need. Cuin himself beheaded many, some of whom still moved and groaned. But he hated so to serve the one he found just outside the fallen walls.

Clarric was dead; the sorrow of slaying him at least was spared Cuin. His blood had spilled in a crimson pool onto the banner of the white hart crumpled beneath him. Nearby lay the lad

Dene, groaning and fighting with the dark. Cuin severed his father's still-warm neck. Then he gathered up the banner; his face was as white as the hart. He wrapped his cousin in its folds and got the youth up before him on the roan. The wyverns and their cloaked allies had stopped within the ruined wall. Cuin rode slowly up the crooked path, with warriors plodding on either side.

He thought he might never come out of the gloom, that Pel had shadowed the earth. It was not until he noted the gleaming orb overhead that he realized he had emerged into the clearer darkness of night. Fléssa winged out of it to meet him, but he sent her flapping away. He wanted no companion, not even the bird.

The army camped all around the rim of the pit. As soon as he could, Cuin left his young cousin in the care of the healers and wandered blindly away. Presently he came to where three men conferred around a fire. Kael and Dacaerin only stared, but Bevan jumped up to meet him.

"Cuin!" he exclaimed. "Where have you been? I feared for you!" Seeking an explanation, he glanced at the rumpled mass in Cuin's arms and smiled wryly. "You need not have taken pains for that. Whatever the hands that made it, 'tis but cloth."

Dazedly Cuin became aware that he still carried the banner of the white hart. "Ay," he replied slowly, "but my father's blood is on it."

Amidst utter silence Bevan took it from him and spread it wide. A broad, bright red stain colored the body of the running deer. "Then shall it have the more honor," Bevan whispered. "What news is this, Cuin?"

"Is Clarric dead?" Dacaerin demanded.

"Ay," Cuin replied dully, "dead and headless." He turned and walked aimlessly away into the night. Bevan came after him.

"Go back," Cuin said.

"I would not leave you in your need," Bevan told him softly.

"Go back to your captains." Cuin faced him without warmth. "I need no living comfort this night."

He strode away again, and Bevan stood and watched him go. Sometime after the setting of the moon, when all the camp was silent with exhausted sleep, Cuin wandered to the bedside of Dene Dale's son and found him also waking.

"How goes it?" Cuin asked with something of gentleness in his voice.

"I shall be well," the lad replied bitterly. "I wish that I had died; it would be better honor. I turned to defend him, but a sword pierced my shoulder behind."

"He went cleanly," Cuin muttered.

"Ay," the lad answered shakily; quiet tears wet his face. Cuin turned away and went to look at the night sky with dry and burning eyes. The heir of Wallyn wept gently in his bed, but Cuin Clarric's son could not weep.

CHAPTER THREE

The next day passed in heavy silence. Looking down into the barren distances of the Pit, guards could see the shattered walls and Pel's priests rummaging amongst the bodies. Nothing else chanced.

When Bevan met with his counselors that day, Cuin was there, with Flessa on his shoulder. His face was pale and hard. Bevan glanced at him inquiringly.

"I shall be well," he replied to the look, "when we have set Pel and his priests on a spear's end. Curse that mantled coward! Where is he? Why does he not show himself and fight?"

Bevan half-smiled, a mirthless grimace. "He fights hard enough for my taste, Cuin! But as for that formless flesh of his, why should he risk it, when he need only keep to his adamant walls? Small wonder he waited so peaceably for our attack."

"Then you have thought of no way to break the keep," Kael said.

"I have thought of no way. Pel's power holds all things of that Pit to his will; the very light accedes to him. He is strong with the strength of ages, and I am young and half-spent." Bevan spoke without self-pity, but even in his own misery Cuin had noted how weariness tightened his comrade's face.

"Moreover," Bevan continued, "the stone of the keep is stolen from the inner depths. It is the very bones of earth. No weapon can match it for potency."

"The gates are of wood," Dacaerin remarked.

"They are protected with runes of ancientest power. Pel Blagden can turn all good things to evil use, it seems."

"Fire will break wood or stone," Cuin said flatly.

"I have never had much dealing with red fire," Bevan answered slowly. "Yet there is truth in what you say, Cuin. Fire is a power even ancienter than earth."

"Fire will destroy all that is to be gained," Dacaerin objected.

Bevan raised his eyebrows. "What greater gain than the destruction of Pel? Yet have no fear for the treasures, my lord." Bitter amusement was in Bevan's glance. "I warrant you they will be stored below; the wyverns show that. Such heavy creatures of darkness live only in the bowels of earth. Pel's stronghold must be a gateway to the regions beneath."

"I do not like that!" Kael exclaimed wryly. "What fell foes might await us there?"

"Strange things, indeed, but not entirely evil. Dwarfs, perhaps, and cold-drakes and other delvers in the inner lands. And perhaps jewels, for which they seek." Bevan almost smiled as he cocked an eye toward Dacaerin. The result was what he expected.

"It is settled then," Pryce said eagerly. "To-morrow we go with torches—"

"Nay, tonight," Bevan told him. "Night is the time for fire and shadows. Moreover, we will use no torches. Need-fire has virtue against evil things, with which man makes very free."

"It will take hours!" Dacaerin protested. "And how can we spare men to tend such fires?"

"My people are far cleverer with fire than with fighting," the King of Romany spoke up serenely. "Let us tend the fires."

"Still, it does not seem wise to take the slower way if a faster way will serve," Kael said worriedly. "What do you say, Cuin?"

"I say let it take until dawn if it must!" Cuin's speech burst from him. "I hope we can slay every heartless lackey of the lot in that time; for slay them we must, soon or late. Would you leave such as them to walk the earth?"

"Look," said Bevan, while Cuin's words still rang on the air. He pointed northward. A marching host raised the dust of the distant plain; above them floated the ship emblem of Firth.

"There are your men," Bevan added quietly.

The Firthola tramped in a hundred strong. Tall, blond-braided men they were, palely shining like the surface of the deep. They had moored their boats under the shadowing Forest of the dark river, and had come south in two long marches by land. That afternoon they rested, and by evening they were more than ready to fight.

In dim twilight Bevan led his warriors down the crooked road and steep slopes once again. Cuin rode at his side, and Kael, bearing the bloodied banner of the white hart. Behind the mounted defense of Kael's retinue, the tribesmen

of Romany led their shaggy ponies, each with a
heavy load of firewood. Pryce Dacaerin headed the
wide ranks of foot fighters that pressed after them.

Bevan's face was white and taut. "I have grieved
you," Cuin murmured as they rode. Bevan shook
his head.

"Death grieves me," he replied softly. "There
is that in this place, Cuin, which could put an
end to death, if we can free it. . . . But too late
on Clarric's behalf."

The gloom of Pel's making hung thickly on
every movement, though its darkness was lost
in the darkness of night. Bevan shone through it
palely, like a candle descending a darkened stair.
At the ruined walls the servants of the mantled
lord waited. In eerie blackness battle was joined.
The priests of Pel numbered far fewer than for-
merly, but they were still plentifully sufficient to
hold the small space of the tower.

"Horsemen to me!" Bevan shouted.

The mounted men rallied around him and
drove like a wedge into the courtyard. Cuin
fought with reckless passion, venting his hatred
and despair on the dark cloaked figures that
swarmed before his feet. At his side Bevan's
golden sword killed with darting precision; no
man could say which comrade felled more. Bevan and Cuin each slew like six men.

In the space they cleared the gypsy tribesmen
prepared for the making of need-fire, that most
potent of fires which springs unbegotten from
the heart of wood itself. Between piles of seasoned fuel they laid a log in which they had carved
a hole, and in the hole they fitted a post topped
with a wheel and ropes. Post and log were of

that most puissant of woods, the oak; but the kindling was of silvery, mystic beech.

While the battle toiled around them, the sons of Romany whirled the upright post, wielding the ropes quickly but with steady rhythm. Powder formed around the post, and presently it began to smoke and glow. While the men still swayed with their ceaseless twirling, the King of Romany approached and shredded bark onto the smoking powder. Tiny flames shot up.

"My lord Bevan!" the gypsy King shouted.

Bevan turned from the combat. The others closed ranks to defend him, but there was little need; already the priests of Pel shrank from the smoke of the infant fire. Bevan spread his hands over its brightening glow and chanted words of blessing.

"*Bellet en soldis,*" he whispered, "*shalde mir nillende es olettyn whe solistet than dilbyst nelltes.*" ["Child of the sun, help us destroy those things that would dishonor your sister Darkness."]

The fire licked its way up the upright post. The gypsies rested their efforts and let their ropes feed the flames. They heaped on wood, and soon the blaze roared man-high and bathed the gloomy courtyard in its scarlet light. The priests of Pel gave way before it, hastily fleeing into the keep. Men cheered and pressed after them, but in vain they battered the gates with their swords; wood and iron held fast.

"Bowmen!" Bevan cried.

The men who walked the fringes of the western Forest were skilled in the shooting of arrows. They tipped their shafts with flame and sent them winging like bright birds through the black sky, arching them into narrow barred windows.

Bevan himself took a fiery brand and rode with
it to the gates. Stretching to his fullest height,
he spoke to it and held it against the ancient
rune of protection carved overhead; then he hurled
it through the pikes into the inner darkness.
Within he heard footfalls as the unmade men
scattered from before it.

Straw and rushes that line a stony floor will
blaze if the defenders fear to prevent it. Presently the upper windows of Pel's stronghold
showed red. Bevan's warriors cheered and piled
flaming sticks against the gate; already it felt
warm from fire within. Soon fire scorched up the
flanks of the hulking tower and leapt like dragon
tongues from its gate. In moments the hard walls
were cloaked in flames whose searing heat drove
the attackers back as Pel's priests could not. Near
the gate the blood-darkened oak smoked sullenly, then flared like a giant torch. Its sparks
fed the furnace that once had been called Pel's
tower. Within the roaring heart of the fire, stones
cracked and tumbled, the iron bars of the gate
twisted and snapped like sticks. No screams could
be heard above the tumult of the flames, so perhaps the unmade men went voicelessly to their
doom. From time to time a scarcely human figure
toppled through the glare, and dark cloaks rose
in bits of ash to join the gore-crows above.

The most embittered of the attackers danced
and cheered to see the unmade men shrivel in
the flames. Others turned away in sickness. Bevan sat his steed and watched quietly. Beside him
Cuin also gazed speechlessly at the fire, spent and
shaken by the force of hot fury that surpassed
even his own.

"Nothing of flesh can live in that," he whispered at last.

"Still I feel a foreboding of evil yet to come," Bevan murmured.

Dacaerin strode up to them, his hair flaming as red as the tower. "What now?" he growled. "We cannot stand here watching a fire all night."

"We can sit," retorted Bevan. "Set a guard, Dacaerin, and let the others rest and sleep. And as for the need-fire, let no one think to quench it, but let it burn out of itself."

"I will take a post of guard," Cuin said.

"Nay, Cuin, sleep," Bevan urged. "I am likely to have dire need of you on the morrow."

"I cannot sleep," Cuin told him.

"If you will let me," Bevan replied gently, "I can bring you sleep."

"Nay," Cuin answered heavily, "this is a path I must walk myself, Bevan. . . ." He turned away to stand his guard, a steely straight figure against the glare of flame.

With the dawn a shower of rain came and cooled the stones somewhat, sending white clouds of steam into the dispersing gloom. By mid-morning the ruins of Blagden loomed fireless and bleak in the gray filtered light of the Pit. The charred and ragged stump of the oak jutted from the lifeless shale. Not even bones of the dead remained near what had been the keep. Only its stones crouched in their lair like a huge lowering animal, and the black void of the gateway gaped like its maw.

With Cuin beside him Bevan strode to the ominous arch. Kael and Dacaerin followed close behind, with their trusted retainers. They all filed into the blackened hall, peering about in

the dim light of arrow slots and twisting cracks
between the stones. Bevan moved surely even in
the murky shade. He summoned them to a broad
stone stairway descending to depths below even
the depth of the eerie Pit. With swords in hand,
soft feet and straining ears, they started down it.

Some priests of Pel had sought refuge here.
Their cloaked bodies littered the steps like giant
crumpled bats. All were dead; the warriors made
sure of each of them as they passed. Presently
the stairway ended, not in dungeons but in a
cavern sculpted by no hand of man. Sinuous
stone curved down to a distance where showed a
glow of red. Bevan raised his flickering sword.

"Wyverns?" Cuin whispered, for no one spoke
but to whisper in those inner parts.

"Duv knows."

Tensely they all stalked down the curling corridor, past more corpses of Pel's cloaked dead.
The bodies clustered thickly, but beyond the curve
of the cavern there were no more. Bare, damp
stone showed plainly in a liquid, ruddy light.

The glow came from a lake like a pool of blood,
with a surface of viscid scarlet and black, con-
gealed depths. Bevan led his company to its
brink, but scarcely had they set foot on its
sculpted bank when the battle-hardened warriors shrieked and ran shaking away. Terrible
serpents most of them feared, things of horror
that no man could withstand, though some were
frightened by more personal demons. Pryce Dacaerin screamed and fled, from what he would
never say. Kael dropped his sword clattering to
the stone, and Cuin cried out and covered his
eyes. Clarric was coming at him out of the bloody
pool, a mutilated Clarric carrying his severed

head; sorrow and reproach were in its sunken gaze. "I had to!" Cuin whimpered.

He felt an arm around him, a warm touch not of this deathly place. "Cuin," Bevan asked, "what is the matter? I see nothing."

"Horror surpassing nightmare." Cuin forced himself to look once more. Clarric still faced him; the vessels pulsed and poured in his severed neck. Cuin stumbled away, catching hold of Bevan like a terrified child. "Let us get hence!" he gasped.

"We must go around," Bevan said.

"I cannot withstand it!" Kael moaned, trembling where he still stood by his dropped sword.

"Then go back with all honor," Bevan told him kindly. "Tell the others to fall back from the Pit; there is no work for them here. Only let our horses be left, mine and Cuin's,—that is, if he goes with me."

"I go with you," Cuin panted like one in physical pain. "But let it be quickly!"

So Cuin was led around the stone rim of the pool, blindly and faltering in his blindness, clutching tightly to Bevan's warm and luminous hand. Presently he felt the horror fade behind him and was able to look around once more. Ever downward they went. The cavern had broadened to a sloping stone hall with many twisting passages leading away. Cuin started; wyverns puffed and woofed from their caves, but they jumped back from the flash of Bevan's sword. Bevan hesitated in the center of the hall, testing the air to all sides.

"What is it?" Cuin asked.

"Pel," Bevan replied abruptly, striding into the darkness to his left. "Hurry, Cuin!"

But they need not have hurried, for the mantled

lord awaited them. Tall and shapelessly dark, he stood before the red light of coals. On the glowing fire shone the giant golden vessel, Coradel Orre. Piled around it were many treasures, but topmost and chiefest among them was a silver crown with shapely tapered rays: essence of gentle white light it seemed, even in this fiery red place. The very walls glowed red and warm with depth. This small cave was indeed the deepest haven of Pel's den, and his treasure chamber, and it was here that he chose to make his stand.

"My lord Pel!" Bevan called sardonically. "Well met at last!"

"And well met, landless Prince," Pel replied coolly. "You have lost your loyal servitors, it seems." His voice was deep and smooth, breathless as the hush before a storm. No mouth moved in the black shadow of his hood; no eyes met theirs. Cuin would have preferred even the most baleful of stares to that form of nothingness. But Bevan seemed unmoved.

"By the great wheel, I still have one friend left to me," he answered placidly. "He will second me. Are you ready, Pel?"

From the flowing shadows of his cloak, the evil god produced a long black sword. No hand showed where he held it; the hilt disappeared into his gaping sleeve. "Have at you," he said tonelessly.

Bevan raised Hau Ferddas. Like a golden flame it lighted that stony place, but even it could not light the shadow that should have been Pel's face. Suddenly Cuin stepped forward. All fear and sickly horror had left him; he had found his deepest strength.

"Bevan," he said urgently, "your father lives,

but mine is dead. Mine is the blood-right; let me
have the vengeance."

Startled, Bevan glanced at him, measuring his
resolve. Cuin was weary, but filled with courage
and a need Bevan could not deny him.

"Then use the blade which is your birthright,"
Bevan said softly. "But you'll not get much blood
from that fellow, Cuin!"

Bevan proffered the jeweled hilt of the legendary sword, and Cuin took it quickly as their
enemy inched nearer. But as his hand closed
around the heavy weapon, Cuin felt a surge of
power such as he had never known. It was as if
a god had entered into him. Strange words he
shouted: *"To nessa laif Elwestrand!"* ["For the
sake of sweet Elwestrand!"] He cried out, and
then he rushed upon the mantled lord.

Pel Blagden gave way before him like air; yet
like air he remained. Cuin had never met so elu-
sive a foe. The golden sword in his hand struck
with eagle power and swiftness, but to no avail.
Among the dark folds of Pel's garments and
hood it met with nothingness. Yet Pel's sword was
real; more than once Cuin caught its crashing
force on his blade. Perplexed, he took up the
posture of defense, studying his adversary. But
then he became aware that Bevan was not idle.
The black-haired Prince stood with his hands on
Coradel Orre, and his face was taut with strain.

The mantled lord must have seen him also. He
lunged past Cuin, but Hau Ferddas flew to prevent him as Cuin stumbled forward in desperate
haste. Doggedly he beat back the nothingness
that was Pel, taking hard blows in the process.
His only concern now was to stay between Bevan
and the foe. All thoughts of vengeance or victory

had left him; he only hoped to stand his ground. Hau Ferddas darted constantly to defend him; as long as he could lift it in his tiring arms he would be well. . . . From time to time he glimpsed Bevan. Though the Prince did not move, yet he trembled with exertion; utmost effort parted his lips and tightened his glistening face. Cuin took a blow on his sword-hilt that staggered him, then straightened to thrust at what should have been his enemy's throat. A cut, a parry, a response—

A rending crash sounded through the place, fearful and sudden as doom. Stunned by the noise, Cuin dropped his guard. But it did not matter. His enemy had crumpled to the stone with a hoarse cry that echoed to the distances of inner earth; centuries of dying were in that cry. Cuin stared. For a flickering instant he thought he saw an ancient, ancient face and wizened hands. A wolf, or a carrion bird. . . . He could not recall the face, he saw only bones—dust?—nay, a formless heap of cloth. Dazed, he turned to Bevan.

But Bevan could not help him. The Prince lay as still as death. The mighty basin of Coradel Orre had shattered, and Bevan was sprawled among its shards of red gold studded with pearls. Cuin sank to his knees beside him and called his name, turned the limp body with his hands. Bevan did not stir; yet there was no wound that Cuin could see.

Some breath of earth seemed to move through the place, an almost soundless stirring, and suddenly Cuin felt a need for greatest haste. He slung Bevan over his shoulders and snatched up the golden sword and silver crown. As quickly as he could, he toiled back the way they had come. In the great cavern the wyverns were barking and

bounding about in wild agitation. From a directionless distance Cuin could hear an echo of rum-
bling, like the first mutterings of an underground
storm.

Up the long reaches of the sloping cavern he
hurried. Panting under his burden, he scarcely
noticed that the crimson pool no longer frightened him, though it still glowed bright as flame.
As he reached the narrower corridor he felt the
stone tremble under his feet, and he broke into
a painful run. All around him the earth was
filled with growling and grating noise. Cuin leaped
up the steps with pounding heart and sped through
the fire-blackened great hall to the gate. The
horses were tethered nearby, his roan and Bevan's dapple-gray. Gasping with exertion, he slung
Bevan over the roan and slashed the tethers of
both horses.

Even as he got up behind Bevan he could see
the gray shale of Blagden's barren slopes come
sliding gently to the bottom. The courtyard shook.
The gray steed whinnied in fright and dashed
away up the twisting road to the top. Cuin sent
the roan after it as quickly as his burden would
let him. Far above he could see Flessa circling
like a speck of fire. Some few hundred feet above
the ground she might be, but she was a mile and
more above him.

The roan ran valiantly, though he snorted in
terror. Halfway up, the road suddenly dropped
from before his hooves; he leaped the gap and
galloped on. Cuin shut his eyes and begged as
he had not begged in all his life: "Mothers, help
us!" Far rather would he have faced a score of
swords than be buried alive. But when he looked
again they were near the rim; indeed, the rim

slid to meet them. The roan scrambled over the
moving ground and ran wildly amidst an army of
gaping, frightened men, until at last it limped
to an exhausted stop beside the lathered dapple-
gray.

Cuin sat and gazed open-mouthed at the abyss
from which he had just come. The ruined fortress was gone, vanished into red depths like a
vast gullet. As he watched, the stones drew closer
like a purse, twisting to tightness. Then the rest
of the Pit moved sickeningly before his eyes; the
substance of it seemed to bubble and roil. Upward
and upward it crept, like broth in a pot. The land
shook; men fell to the ground and cried out in
fear. Cuin got Bevan down from the roan, shield-
ing him with his arms. But as suddenly as sunshine all was over. Flessa swooped down and
serenely landed on Cuin's shoulder. Where the Pit
had been was now a field of rubble, level with the
surrounding plain. Earth had reclaimed her
wounded breast and stolen bones.

A hubbub of talk sprang up as men questioned
and reassured each other. Dacaerin strode up to
Cuin.

"Is that one alive?" he demanded.

It was a question Cuin had pushed far back
in his thoughts. Bevan scarcely seemed to breathe;
but his hands were warm. "I do not know,"
Cuin said numbly.

Kael pushed up and held his burnished breastplate to Bevan's face. Breath moistened it. "He
lives," Kael declared. "Indeed, I see no mark on
him. What has hurt him?"

Cuin could not say; sorrow and weariness had
fogged his mind. They got Bevan to the tents of
the healers, where they put him in a bed, but

they could think of nothing more to do for him. Sunset came, and dark, but Bevan did not stir. Cuin sat by him through the night, his mind frozen in despair. The young lord of Wallyn waited on them both.

In the darkness before dawn one of Dacaerin's men came.

"Something flits white above the place that was the Pit," he told Cuin in a low, shaky voice. "I do not dare awaken my lord Dacaerin for such a ghost; he is full of spleen. But we are frightened, lord. Will you come?"

Only the terror in the man's voice moved Cuin to sluggish response. Leaving Bevan in Dene's care, he trudged out to the lines of guard and beyond, not much caring what he might meet. But as the white form took shape in the night, new warmth surged through Cuin. It was the hart.

"Wait but a moment!" he told it absurdly, and ran to get the dapple-gray.

He gathered up Bevan, blankets and all, and cradled him in his arms as he rode into the dark. The horse faded from the sight of the guards like a cloud in the night, following a dim white star. The stag ran before Cuin and the steed, stopping and circling impatiently at their slowness. Westward over the sky-broad land it led them, until in the dusk of dawn it came to a place where a single silver tree pierced the plain to court the sky. Here Cuin laid Bevan down, and the creatures nestled nearby. Cuin sat and waited. Yet he could not tell, so deep was his sleepless despair, whether he had brought his liege here to live or to die.

Dawn turned to paler gray and pearly white

and gold. When it had grown to bright gold, Bevan stirred and sat up. "What am I doing here?" he muttered, poking his blankets.

Cuin knelt before him dazedly. "How do you feel?" he whispered.

"How should I feel?" Bevan's mouth twisted in gentle jest. "Well enough."

"Sweet Prince, I thought I had lost you too!" Cuin choked, and he clenched himself against his store of unspent tears. But Bevan touched him, and he wept like a child. There was no mystic power of healing in the hands that held him, no argent glow, but only the comfort of mortal friendship. It was enough. Cuin softened into quietude and settled into sleep. Bevan leaned against the pearly tree and pillowed Cuin's head on his arm. Flessa brooded above them, and nearby the white hart dozed.

Thus it was that Ellid found them, when she walked that way in the morning.

CHAPTER FOUR

"So I have failed," Bevan told Ellid later that day. "Coradel Orre is destroyed."

She regarded him quizzically, scarcely understanding. "The news I hear is that you have won a great victory! Pel Blagden is destroyed, he and all his works. The son of the immortals has triumphed over an immortal enemy."

"A god of dust. He would have been but a mortal did not the power of Coradel Orre sustain him. As it would have sustained me." Bevan sighed. "Now that it is gone, I must truly accustom myself to a mortal fate."

She stared at him. "A mortal and a King! Your lot could be worse, Prince of Eburacon!"

"Ay, Eburacon indeed is left to me." Bevan's gaze softened. "The fair fountains and golden orchards of Eburacon! Let us go there after we are wed, Ellid—just the two of us for a few days, as we were before. But then I will bring rest to the guardian shades, and let in my people, to make it my court city." He stopped, his smile fading to a frown. "If my strength returns, I can do that! Right now I am but a plodder on the earth, like other men. It is strange and terrible to be made so lightless. I feel like an empty shell."

"Surely you will soon be better," Ellid comforted him. "Everyone is spent after such a struggle. Look at Cuin."

For Cuin still slept, sprawled with childlike abandon beneath the silver tree. Bevan winced with pity for him.

"He has sorrowed," he said, "and he has bled, and at the last he saved me, so men say, together with the sword and the Argent Crown, no less! Any one of the three would have been wonder enough. Your cousin is a marvel among men, Ellid."

"A marvel of stupidity!" Cuin stood up and shook himself, then ambled over to join them. "That very night I should have had you to the holy grove, Bevan."

"What, and my lady here?" Bevan smiled at him. "The hart led you aright, Cuin. Have you slept well?"

"Ay," Cuin answered slowly, "except that still Pel's vile mockery of my father troubles my inward sight. The thing in the bloody pool."

"It was not Clarric, only a semblance of Pel's making," Bevan told him softly. "You know that, do you not? I grieve that I have no better help to give you . . ."

Cuin shrugged. "Time will take the sting from it. But may I never forget the glory of Hau Ferddas!" His brown eyes lighted with wonder. "That is a weapon men would die for. What were the strange words it tore from me?"

"*To nessa laif Elwestrand,*" Bevan murmured. "For the sake of sweet Elwestrand. I do not know what it means, but it went through me like a sword."

"Even so should I be skewered for folly!" Cuin struck himself. "I left the golden sword—and the crown—with mine uncle Pryce Dacaerin!"

"Why, what is the harm in that?" Ellid stared in puzzlement. "My father is no thief."

"Nay, but you have not laid hands on Hau Ferddas, Ellid." Cuin faced her squarely. "It cozens the will to power. I was a fool and thrice a fool to let it out of my sight."

"You were sunk in sorrow and weary to the bone," Bevan said to him. "Moreover, do not think so badly of your uncle. He has done valiant service; I can find no fault with him this day."

"Still, I would return forthwith," Cuin muttered.

"Eat and we shall go."

So they rode back to what had been Blagden in the golden light of late afternoon, with Cuin on a borrowed horse and Ellid on the dapple-gray before Bevan. Cuin and Bevan gaped as they drew near, but Ellid only smiled; she had not sent messengers for naught. To a man the warriors stood ranked upon the plain awaiting them, and at a signal they raised their gold-decked sword-arms with a mighty shout.

Ellid dropped lightly to the ground and went aside with Cuin. Bevan stood alone in the clearing, still and arrow-straight. Pryce Dacaerin strode up and bowed before him ceremoniously. "My lord of Eburacon," he addressed him, "there are those here who would swear their fealty to you this day."

"The crown!" Kael shouted. "Let us swear to him whom we have crowned our High King!"

Dacaerin turned and tried to frown him into silence, but Kael met his stare, grinning happily. "Though none of us is worthy of such noble office, to crown him, indeed," he added roguishly.

"All of you are worthy," Bevan said in his soft, melodious voice, which was heard by all.

"Then let us all have a hand in it!" Kael cried. "Page, ho!"

Young Dene of Wallyn came forward with the silver crown on a cushion; men strained and shoved to touch it as it passed. "Now, my lords!" Kael directed. "Nay, my liege, you need not kneel. . . ." With many hands they placed on Bevan the Argent Crown of Eburacon; their arms encircled him. Dacaerin glowered as Cuin stood watching in delight. "Poor Uncle!" he whispered to Ellid. "He had hoped to have this honor to himself."

"The sword!" exclaimed the King of Romany. "Where is his sword?"

"Boy!" Pryce ordered harshly.

Dene brought Hau Ferddas wrapped in a cloth. Bevan reached for it and raised it high; it flashed like a flame in the light of the setting sun. The warriors murmured in awe, then burst into a cheer. Kael helped Bevan gird on the sword, and kissed him. Then he knelt before him.

"Liege, let me be the first to pledge you my faith."

"You are dear to me," Bevan told him tenderly. "But let Cuin come to me as well."

"What?" Cuin smiled at Bevan from his place aside. "I am no lord."

"You will be, when we have found a holding worthy of you." Bevan stretched out his hand. "Come."

Dazedly, Cuin obeyed him. Kneeling with hands cupped within his King's, he huskily recited the ancient oath of fealty: ". . . to honor and defend . . . support and uphold . . . in steadfast loyalty. . . ." When he had done he stood at Bevan's side while the other lords swore in their turn, binding themselves by whatever gods they held dear. Pryce Dacaerin was among the last, and he swore by blood.

When the last lord stood, Cuin raised his blade. "Long live Bevan High King!" he shouted, and the others took up the cry. The men broke ranks and surged forward to see and touch, but Ellid was ahead of them. She kissed Bevan on the lips, there under the golden sky, and the warriors cheered them riotously. Dene raised the standard of the white hart as high as his young arms could hold it. Ellid looked where it floated, and her face went white as death.

"What is that stain?" she whispered.

"Noble blood." Bevan had an arm around her, gazing at her from under his crown that was like a silver sun. "Clarric's crimson can but do it honor."

"It is like an omen! I cannot bear to look at it!" Ellid hid her face, shivering. "Take it away."

"Put it hence, lad," Bevan said gently to Dene, and turned toward the setting sun. The warriors were scattering toward their campfires, rejoicing and looking for ale. A few lords lingered near.

"Will you go north now, Kael?" Bevan asked.

"Not until you are wed!" the black-braided King exclaimed. "I would not fail to honor you at that feast."

"Let them be wed at Caer Eitha," Pryce put in, "and thus your travel will be shortened."

"Nay," Bevan said flatly. "I will lodge that night within no walls of man. It is the fairest of seasons; let our bed be where the blessing of earth can reach us."

"You cannot mean to take her to the Forest!" Dacaerin objected. "There is no place for feasting beneath that shade."

"There is room and reason for feasting on the Downs," Cuin remarked dreamily. "In all this realm which I have seen, no place is so fair as where the grassland looks down upon Welas. Everything there is sunlit green and golden, and the meadowlarks sing through the day."

"Then you should build a fair city there, Cuin," Bevan charged him, "and call it Laveroc, the city of larksong. May we wed on your domain, Cuin?"

"I believe my cousin would be well pleased by it," Cuin answered softly, and Ellid smiled at him.

So the company traveled gently westward. It was Kael and his diminished band, the gypsies and the Firtholas, Bevan and Cuin and Pryce Dacaerin with his retinue, including Ellid and Eitha in their closely-curtained horse-litter. A few other lords rode with them, but most of the southern lords pressed quickly home, to return to the wedding feast with wives and gifts. Though the warm weather was nearing its height, there was no raiding in the land. For the first summer in living memory crops went untrampled, cottages unburned. The peasants thanked their gods for the prosperity that seemed assured, now that their lords had turned their attention to feasting rather than fighting. Folk deemed that this was the decree of the new-crowned King, but they were only partly right. A spirit of peace hung over Isle, for friendships had been formed beside the dreadful Pit of Blagden.

Always beside the High King rode Cuin; Cuin Falconer men called him because of the bird that was ever on his shoulder or circling above his steed. Many lords looked on him with favor, for he was quiet, courteous and valiant, and a right way of seeing shone in his deepset brown eyes. But for Bevan the King his comrade they felt nothing less than awe: for they saw that he had leveled the Pit by the power of his mystic will, and had brought all of Pel's works to ruin with his shining hands and sword.

In a score of easy days the company reached the place of laverocs and set up their encampment. Tents were pitched; Ellid and Eitha embellished them with bright pennons and ribbons. Cooking pits were dug and lined with stones. Many of the men departed to the Forest, half a day's journey away, to bring in game for the feast. Cuin went, but Bevan stayed with Ellid.

The sunny vistas of the Downs pleased Ellid anew each day. She never tired of gazing about her. "Cuin was right," she told Bevan. "This place is a delight to me."

"He knows you well," Bevan said softly.

Soon the other chieftains arrived, and the soft billows of the Downs became brightly decked with pavilions and fluttering flags. Glossy steeds grazed round about; sleek-haired women strolled in groups and chattered around the fires at night. The hunters returned, and Cuin kept Bevan company, for Ellid was busy with private preparations. Bevan was restive, for the attentions of the assembly galled him. "Praise Duv this will soon be over," he muttered.

"And what of your court?" Cuin teased him. "You are King now for your life's span! Would you spend it in a cave, then?"

"Ay, well," Bevan said heavily, "the night at least is left to me." And when dusk brought the fires to full glow he would be gone, a wanderer in the dark where no one followed him.

The wedding was set for the time of the new moon: a propitious season, the priests said. Priests of every sort were present to nod and be wise before the wedded pair. Bevan ignored them, giving them his assent only by his silence. But on an eve of the dark of the moon came messengers he could not ignore. Three dark, stocky men on scarecrow ponies forded the Gleaming River from Welas. Pryce Dacaerin spoke something of their foreign tongue, and he named their request to Bevan.

"They come from Owen of Twyth, he who is chieftain by the first mountain of the sea," Pryce said. "He wishes certain assurances of your intent these years to come, and he desires an emmissary to set the terms of mutual peace."

"He need not worry," Bevan remarked crossly. "I am no warmonger."

"He has heard of your prowess," Cuin smiled. "I will go."

"Nay, let someone else go. Or at least let it wait until after the wedding."

"In truth," Cuin told him quietly, "I would rather not be here for the wedding."

So silent was Cuin's pain, when he looked on Ellid's happiness, that Bevan had almost forgotten it. Remorse gripped him as he met Cuin's eyes, and he failed to reckon with danger.

"Go then with all blessing," he said hastily,

"and do not forget to return quickly." He clasped his comrade's hand, but could think of nothing more to say. Then he strode off into the moonless night.

At dawn Cuin left for Welas on his roan, towering above the three swarthy messengers and their runty beasts. Bevan was nowhere to be seen, but Ellid embraced her cousin in farewell. She watched Cuin go with a sorrow she could scarcely explain even to herself. She knew well enough the meaning of his departure, for she felt sure that he had not ceased to care for her. Still, her path had been chosen a year before. What, then, was this anguish that tugged at her heart?

The next day was her wedding day. The taking of a wife was marked by no vows in those times; most often a woman merely made herself a bundle and trudged to her new home. But the wedding of a King was an act of royal policy and a portent of all good to the realm. Moreover, Ellid was Pryce Dacaerin's daughter. The broad lands of his holdings were to be wedded to the budding power of the young High King. Every lord in Isle who had even ten men to command was there for the event. The showing of their gifts made a high heap upon the grassy height of the Downs.

The company gathered upon the rounded promontory that gave view upon hazy distances even unto the ends of Isle, or so it seemed. To the clearing at its flattened apex Ellid stepped. The heavy chains that hung her neck and arms with gold were but a portion of the dowry that Pryce had settled on her. A wreath of wheat was on her head, for fertility, and signs of every god and good omen were stitched in gold upon her dress

of blue, the color of constancy. In her hands she
held coins and cloth, for prosperity. Indeed, she
bore the burden of as many hopes as folk could
find symbol for, and beneath it all she herself
was scarcely Ellid; she was a vessel, the Bride.
Beside her Bevan was weighted as heavily with
sword and robes and crown; he had become no
more Bevan, but an implement, the King. Bride
and King met each other's eyes, but they could
scarcely see each other past the glitter of their
gear.

The priests postured and babbled. Lords pa-
raded their wishes and their wealth. Pryce Dacaerin orated at length. Finally he grasped the girl
and turned her, Bevan took her hand in his, and
that simply all was done. They walked down the
grassy slope to the cooking pits, and their people
trooped behind them. Feasting began and went
on until long after dark. Ale flowed, and many a
bawdy jest was told. Ellid blushed as she ner-
vously picked at her food, but Bevan seemed
scarcely to hear. His face was as pale as the
ermine of his robe, and his dark eyes looked far
eastward, toward Eburacon.

At last the maidens came and, giggling, led
Ellid away. Later the men who were not too
drunk took Bevan in like wise. Kael, reeling up-
roariously, relieved him of his robes; Dacaerin
took the crown and sword. Delightedly, the others
showed him to his tent. He stepped within and
listened to them tramp away.

Ellid lay clad only in her shift upon a high-
piled bed of pillows and quilts. She scarcely
breathed as Bevan came and lay beside her, laid
his hand upon her. There was no warmth in the

hand, no power of passion. From without came the sound of raucous laughter, and Bevan groaned.

"Love," he whispered intensely, "it is all wrong; from beginning to end this day is wrong. I am not I; there is no heart in me; I am a puppet and a shell, as empty as yon black shell of a moon. I could not bed you if all nights were to end this night."

"Ay," she answered dully, "all has come to naught since Cuin went."

"By thunder, you speak truly!" Bevan breathed, and sprang up from the bed. Ellid stopped him with a startled gasp.

"Where are you going?"

"Duv knows! There is healing in the night, even the night of the hollow moon."

"You will shame me!" Ellid cried. "They will look for you here in the morning. Lie with me at least, and let me hold you; perhaps you will find some comfort thus." Tears choked her.

"So, even so," Bevan hastened to assure her, and he laid his supple body close to hers. He pillowed his head on her breast and felt her tears upon his raven-black hair; but there were no tears in Bevan of Eburacon.

Early the next morning, while most of the camp still lay in drunken stupor, Pryce Dacaerin rose and went a-hunting. He took with him bow and spear and a weapon strange for the search of game: the golden sword of Lyrdion, wrapped in a cloth of the dragon device.

He knew quite well where the white hart was to be found, for several times the hunters had seen it haunting the lower reaches of the Forest near the Downs. Always it flitted away far too fast for their pursuit, if such had been their intent. But Pryce Dacaerin was skilled in stealth when stealth would serve his purpose. In the midday of mid-summer, when all creatures of the wilds lie and doze beneath the woven shade, Dacaerin stalked until he saw the gleam of silver antlers above the dappled ferns.

Dacaerin drew his bow until the string touched his ear. The steel head of the yardlong shaft pointed full at the hart's reclining side. But even as the bolt was loosed some nameless finger of fear touched the stag; it leaped up and darted away. Cursing, Dacaerin ran for his horse. Still, he had not entirely missed his game. The knifelike arrow had sliced deep into the hart's leg above the hock. Now the blood-spoor dotted the leaves. East toward Eburacon it led.

Dacaerin's red bay horse was tall and lithe of limb. Swiftly it ran between the trees, with its red-haired master bent to its neck in his eagerness. Through the long hot afternoon Dacaerin rode, and from time to time a flash of white far ahead showed him his quarry. Toward evening he knew that the hart must be growing lame and stiff, for swaying branches told him that it had but lately passed. Yet he frowned, for night drew on relentlessly, and darkness would bring his chase to an end. He spurred the horse to the fastest pace the Forest would allow.

In the gray light of dusk he grasped his spear, left the twisting trail of blood and spurred straight between the trees. Presently he sighted the hart and gave a harsh shout of triumph. Foam flecked its mouth, and its dark eyes stared half-stunned from its delicate face. Dacaerin knew the look;

he had seen it often in man and beast. His prey could not withstand him longer.

Still its failing legs ran as swiftly as his tiring steed; Pryce struggled long to draw abreast of it. It was the last dim moments of twilight when he loosed his spear at last, and the hart staggered and fell with the blow. Then with trembling effort it rose, wrenched itself free of the spear and struggled away. Dacaerin watched it go and was well content. He had seen the bright stain spread on its white flank, and he believed that it could not live for long.

CHAPTER FIVE

Ellid arose her first wedded morn to a husband as distant as her home. Bevan said little to her, but spent the day in council with his lesser lords, settling countless details of tribute and defense. Ellid knew that he was glad of the excuse to busy himself apart from her. Also she suspected he was glad of her father's absence, though she wondered where Dacaerin had gone. Her mother knew nothing, and as the day wore on Eitha passed from wonder to worry, roaming the camp and discreetly inquiring after her husband. But if anyone had seen him go they held their tongues, for it did not do to question the ways of Pryce Dacaerin.

That evening Ellid and Bevan sat again with the company at the fires and ate the cold meats of yesterday's feast. Bevan reached for her hand.

"Tomorrow we will ride toward Eburacon," he whispered for her ear only. "Just ourselves, Love. All will yet be well with us—"

Ellid gasped and caught at his hand as he nearly toppled into the fire. Bevan was stricken like one felled by an invisible blow, and though waking he was speechless with pain. Men shouted and brought wine; women plied him with plasters and rubs. Still he crouched stiff and trembling with agony. Kael and some others got him gently to the high-piled bed, where Ellid and Eitha stayed with him. Through that night he lay wide-eyed and shaking; nor did Dacaerin return.

The next day dawned as golden as every day seemed to be on the Downs. Ellid could have cursed the sunshine that mocked her misery. Bevan lay in ceaseless suffering through the day, and though he sometimes gasped out a word, he could tell nothing of what ailed him. Ellid held his hands and stroked his head, but she knew that she scarcely eased him. The others sat idly and waited in anxious gloom, as if there had been an omen of disaster; for no reason Kael doubled the guard. Folk scanned the horizons to no avail. Dacaerin did not come, and nothing chanced except that, near nightfall, Bevan groaned and closed his eyes. Ellid rushed to him. He still breathed, but he seemed to know no more, and she was glad of it.

On the following morning Ellid sent men out to seek news of her father, for though Eitha said nothing her eyes were rimmed with red. At nightfall the party returned; they had scouted a great circle, miles around, and seen no sign but this: in the southern reaches of the Forest they had found a spent arrow and a bow. Ellid took the things without a word, but a strange fear clenched her heart, and she sat beside her stricken liege that night with cold dread for her cloak.

Cuin had not traveled even a day with his taciturn companions before he learned to distrust them. He bore them no grudge because they did

not speak his tongue, but it troubled him that
they snarled and would not meet each other's eyes.
Yet for two days they rode without incident, and
for two nights he slept lightly and was undis-
turbed. They forded the Gleaming River and
wended deep into the folding valleys that rose to
the hills and mountains of Welas. This was a
fair green country, but densely wooded, and Cuin
saw few folk. His three bear-like guides took him
southward, toward the mountains that rimmed
the sea. In the foothills the soil was thinner and
more easily worked. There Owen of Twyth had
established his domain.

On the third night Cuin went early to his
blanket, for he was tired from riding and sick at
heart. He had tried not to think of Bevan and
Ellid, wedded now these two days, but still visions
of their happiness would torment him. He could
not wish them ill, but devoutly he pitied himself,
for well he knew that he would never feel such
joy. Ellid was never to be his, and none other
would he wed, through all his life.

He lay silent but waking until his rough companions were snoring. Then he slipped into fitful
sleep and dreamed a dream that seared his mind.
Ellid was sitting on a green Forest bank, clad only
in her shift. Her tawny hair had grown and fell
softly over her shoulders. Cuin had never seen
her so unadorned and so lovely. The white hart
came and gazed at her with dark and glowing
eyes; then it knelt and couched its antler-crowned
head on her lap. Ellid bent to kiss its mouth. But
as she kissed it a giant red dragon loomed over
them and devoured the hart; the Forest earth was
stained with its blood. Ellid cried out again and
again, but her cries were the piercing cries of a

bird. She beat upon the dragon with her hands; her hands changed to the golden wings of a bird and beat the air. She flew and circled, crying. . . .

Wings of a bird touched Cuin's face. His eyes snapped open as Flessa darted away. For a moment he could not think where he was, but peril rang through him as he stared. In the darkness he saw darker shapes like three stumpy trees that had not been there before. Cuin drew his sword even as he sprang up and kicked the fire for light.

They rushed him quickly, three against one. But they were hacking swordsmen, while he was taller and doubly skilled. He held them off with the length of his arm until he pricked them one by one. Then he gave them each the mercy stroke and sat down to clean his sword. Sleep was fled from him for that night; he did not know what to think. Why would Owen of Twyth set his men to slay an emissary? At worst he had thought they might intend him a painful welcome at his journey's end. But such a pass as this meant nothing, not even as defiance. Perhaps the men were merely robbers; might there be more about? But surely they had chosen a peculiar way to find their game!

Cuin sat through the night with his nerves on edge. By morning he had decided what he must do. Owen of Twyth was a chieftain of fair repute, rough perhaps but not vicious. If these were his men, he deserved to know of them. Moreover, Cuin Kellarth was not one to turn his back on a task. He would travel as emissary to the southlands of Welas and bring back word to his King. Cuin left the bodies of the slain men where they lay, food for gore-crows. But he

loaded their gear on their beasts. Roping the
ponies together, he led off on his roan.

Crazed, many might have called him, to ride
to the holding of a foreign lord with spoils of
three dead men in his train! Indeed, he often
wondered at himself as he went, for he would not
confess the real reason for his journey: that he
could not bear to return to Bevan. Not yet.

It was darkest night, and even the crescent
moon had set, when Kael came to Ellid where she
sat at Bevan's bedside.

"Lady," he told her shakily, "there is a shape of
whiteness on the Downs. I dare say it pertains
to our liege in some way, but I'll not deceive you:
I have not nerve to go near it."

"The hart!" Ellid breathed joyfully, and hurried out at once. The guards huddled together
and pointed to the north. Ellid could see no more
than a white blur in the distance. Swiftly she ran
to meet it, until she was all alone in the night,
and then she stopped with a shudder as terror
froze her where she stood. It was not the hart
that stood before her; it was a woman who carried a bloodstained cloth in her hand.

She was neither old nor young, but agelessly
beautiful; and though her hair was white, it was
the same luminous white as her hands and dress.
Her face glowed as pale, but no line was on it.
She glided rather than walked as she drew near.
Ellid felt faint, for the white ladies of the night
were said to enslave mortals with a word. . . . But
yet the night was Bevan's friend. Ellid forced her
tongue to move.

"What do you want?" she whispered.

"My son," the woman answered in a voice that carried all the music of sorrow.

"Celonwy!" Ellid breathed as all her fear flowed from her. She knew now where she had seen the delicate shading of that face. "Mother," she murmured, and turned to lead her to the tent. The guards scattered before them, and even Eitha gulped and fled. Ellid did not care, for she had heard the love in that melodious voice.

Bevan lay with ashen face and lidded eyes; his body was clenched in pain. The goddess sat and took his head into her arms. She bared his chest, and on it she placed her blood-soaked cloth. She pressed it fervently with her white hands as she raised her face and called out in words that Ellid did not understand.

Bevan stirred, then lay still with deep and easy breathing. A faint glow lighted his cheeks. Shaking, Ellid knelt to touch him. Then with silent tears she reached out to the one who had healed him. Celonwy took her hand and embraced her; a mortal caress, though Ellid could not have said how she knew. Blinking the tears from her eyes, she looked again; it was only a lovely old woman who sat by Bevan's sleeping form.

When Bevan awoke, hours later, it was Ellid's tired face that first met his eyes. He reached out to her hungrily. "Oh, Love, Love," he murmured, and kissed her tenderly; warm comfort flowed through her from his caress. "I am sorry," he whispered.

"Hush," she told him gently. "Look, here is one who you have not seen this year and more."

Bevan looked on a placid white-haired woman he did not know, then looked again as truth struck in. "My mother!" he cried, then choked as he embraced her. "Oh, Mother, you have given yourself over to Death!"

" 'Tis not so fearful a prospect, and high time, too," she said serenely. "Your father went, these many months ago, and he went gladly."

"Death is a fair fellow, some folk say," Bevan replied shakily, "but still I would not meet him yet awhile."

"Nay, for you have the best of life yet to taste, my son." Celonwy smiled. "Therefore, when I knew that you must leave me and blunder into darkest peril, I conjured from you your vitalest spirit and placed it in the keeping of a noble thing, the white hart. And in you I settled some of its feral wanderlust to carry you out of danger. Thus your lives were linked, and so long as either of you lived, the other could not die. 'Twas interference of me, I own it. Twice to my knowledge it has saved you, but some harm has come of it. You could not fully live, fully love or fully sorrow. . . . At your core you were but a wild thing, a wanderer apart from men. And finally it brought you to the misery wherein I found you."

"But what has happened to the hart?" Bevan exclaimed. Ellid's face was taut and white.

"It struggled back to me, terribly wounded by a hunter's spear. Swift of steed and hard of heart must have been he who pursued it. It will be dead now and done with suffering, thanks be. . . . I took some of its blood on a napkin and hastened here to give back to you what I had taken, your veriest heart. I rejoice that you are well now, but I grieve for the passing of a thing so lovely."

"Sorrow be to him who smote it," Bevan muttered.

"We all know who that may be," Eitha spoke

from the entry. Her round chin trembled, but her gentle face was set in hard lines; anguish spoke in that hardness.

Ellid went to her swiftly and put her arms around her. "Mother," she told her softly, "there is no need."

"There is need for me to be a woman and no more a worm. Lass, he is not the man I wed. These months past all concern has gone from him except the cold cunning of power. I know that he wed you to Bevan only so that he could be the father of a Queen. He drove Cuin from us to keep you as his heir. And now he has taken the golden sword."

"What word from Cuin?" Bevan demanded.

"None," Ellid whispered. "He is yet in Welas."

"Then I must ride forthwith." Bevan jumped up to make ready, scattering clothing in his haste. "Find me some food and my gear. . . . Ellid, you would not have me stay when Cuin is in peril?"

"Nay," she answered. "But take Kael with you."

"Nay, I must go alone. I'll take no retainers; this must be no invasion, or I'll have Welas up in arms. Bide here and wait for word."

He kissed her hastily and hugged his mother and was off as fast as the dapple-gray could take him. The camp watched amazed as he disappeared in the distance toward Welas. At the tent flap three women stood: a sorrowing matron, a snowy-haired goddess and a young wife lovely as the dawn. Yet in their fears their three minds were as one.

A week later, after steady travel, Cuin came to Twyth. The tilled land and pastureland climbed sharply to the fortress which was set halfway up the first mountain that soared between Welas and the sea. With his booty in tow Cuin ascended the steep trail to the gates, oblivious to the stares of the peasantry. "Open up!" he shouted in the language of Isle.

The gatekeeper peeped at him and scuttled away. Cuin waited for minutes of rising irritation. "Who goes there?" a voice challenged him at last from within, in the Islendais speech, though haltingly spoken.

What was he to say? He was lord neither of Wallyn nor the lands Dacaerin, but only of a nameless empty plain. "Cuin Falconer," he roared at last, "emissary of Bevan High King in Isle to Owen of Twyth in Welas. I come in peace, though peace has not been my lot. Open up!"

Slowly the gates creaked open, and more hastily Cuin rode in. The one who addressed him in his own tongue was a burly man of middle age. "I am Owen of Twyth," he said warily. "You are welcome, King's Man, for the sake of your liege, whatever might be your business here."

"That is for you to say, lord." Cuin dismounted to address him. "You who sent for me."

The big man's eyes widened. "I sent not!"

"Three short and swarthy fellows came to our camp," Cuin explained laboriously, "requesting an emissary to Twyth with assurances of peaceful intent."

"Gladly would I make treaty of peace with Bevan High King," the chieftain protested, "but I sent no one. Where are these men who used my name?"

"They beset me in the night, like robbers, and I slew them. Those are their beasts and gear."

Owen ran his eye over the horses with polite disdain. "You should have slain them with their masters," he said. "I would be ashamed to keep such nags in my stables."

"I have disturbed you to no purpose, lord," Cuin mumbled. All sense told him that the blunt-spoken man spoke the truth, and sudden trouble stirred in his heart. He vaulted onto his roan.

"You need not go!" Owen exclaimed. "Stay and eat, and we will speak of your liege."

"That was courteously said," Cuin told him. "But I feel a storm of sorrow brewing, lord; some subtle cunning took me from my liege lord's side. I must return to him in all haste. I hope we shall more happily meet again." Cuin raised a hand in salute and spurred toward the gate.

"What of your nags?" the chieftain called after him.

"Feed them to your dogs!" Cuin shouted, and sent his steed plunging down the mountain. He muttered vehemently the while, berating himself, but he did not have much time for the luxury of self-reproach. Scarcely had he entered the woven shade when a red horse and tall red-haired rider moved before him; Pryce Dacaerin blocked his path. Cuin stared, for in his uncle's hand was the great golden sword of Lyrdion.

"Well met, nephew," said Dacaerin harshly.

"So it was you who set them to slay me," Cuin whispered.

Pryce threw back his head and laughed, a cold, dragonish laugh. "Ay, I paid those three to take you, and I knew you would not be sorry to go

with them! But they have botched the task, it
seems, and I must do it myself. I would have
done it before now, could I have torn you away
from that precious Prince of yours—my curse on
you both!"

"Why?" Cuin met his eyes squarely, without
anger or plea. "We have always honored you, my
liege and I, and spoken fairly of you."

"Honored me!" Dacaerin spat the words out with
reptilian virulence; Cuin recoiled from the passion
of his hatred. "Honored me! I have done well that
you have not yet reft me of my lands! You two
have taken all else: my men's loyalty, my wife's
affection, my daughter and my sword! For this
sword is by rights mine, Cuin traitor!" Dacaerin
came closer, brandishing Hau Ferddas before
Cuin's startled face. "I, too, am an heir of the line
of Lyrdion, and were it rightly reckoned the sword
should have been mine, and kingdom and crown
as well!"

Pryce laughed again, and blood was in his
laugh. "But I shall have my own again, Cuin
King's Man; even my daughter shall I have, and
she shall make a King of me."

"All the clans are sworn to vengeance against
an oath-breaker and a shedder of kindred blood,"
Cuin breathed.

"I have broken no oath and shed no kindred
blood!" Dacaerin crowed with cruel triumph. "I
have merely slain a deer, a fair white hart—as I
will slay you who have betrayed me!" Pryce
Dacaerin rushed with treacherous suddenness as
Cuin sat frozen with the despair of his tidings.
But Flessa shot from Cuin's shoulder and beat
her wings against Dacaerin's helm, driving her

talons at his eyes. Furiously the lord swung at her
with his leather-clad fist, knocking her broken to
the ground. Cuin did not see; he had wheeled and
fled.

He knew that he stood no chance against the
mystic force of Hau Ferddas. Swiftly he sent the
roan along the rim of the Forest, but Dacaerin's
steed was as swift after him, forcing him away
from the shelter of the trees. Cuin galloped over
the sparse shoulders of the mountains, vainly
seeking refuge. Something stung his foot, and the
roan lurched. Cuin looked down, even now scarcely able to believe the infamy of his uncle's deeds.
Then he leapt away as his steed fell to earth with
Dacaerin's spear jutting from its side. With a jeer
Pryce spun his bay to run him down.

Like a hunted animal Cuin took to the rocks,
seeking heights where the red horse could not
follow. Panting, he scrambled up toward the
jagged rim of Welas. His youth stood him in good
stead here, and he soon left Dacaerin far behind.
But the blood-spoor of his cut foot marked his
trail. Gasping, he sat to bind it.

That done, he climbed more slowly to a high
defile between two great crags of stone. Once
there he thought to make his way along the
mountainous ridge out of Dacaerin's sight. He
scarcely knew for what he wished to escape. To
wrest the sword from his uncle, at all cost. . . .
But what use was it, if Bevan was dead? Tears
streaked Cuin's cheeks, for Bevan's fate and for
his own folly in leaving him. Painfully he reached
the defile and limped over its peak. But ten steps
farther on he stopped, stunned. A narrow ledge
ran off to his right before coming up against a

wall of stone. Below dropped only sheer cliffs, falling thousands of feet to the unheard crashing of the Western Sea.

Cuin turned, already knowing what he would see. Pryce Dacaerin straddled the defile, looming against the sky. The sea breeze lifted his bright hair like a plume of fire, and the giant sword shone flame-bright in his hand. Fierce exultation lighted his face. Cuin had seen such a fire-crested face before.

"Ay, you're a true King of Lyrdion," he shouted bitterly, and strode to meet him.

What ensued was scarcely to be called a duel. Cuin could not stand against Hau Ferddas, which darted faster than human hand could guide it. Within moments he was driven back to the cliff, and along the ledge to the wall and stood with his back to the rock. Already he bled from a dozen wounds. He held his sword before him; Dacaerin's next blow broke it off in his hand. Cuin tossed the useless hilt into the abyss of the sea and waited for the end.

"So!" Dacaerin mocked. "It seems that I need not be guilty of spilling your heart's-blood, nephew. I have only to nudge you over the edge, thus." He placed the mighty point of the sword at Cuin's side and pressed it like a goad. But Cuin did not budge even as the blade bit into him.

"It will not be so easy, Uncle!" he panted between teeth clenched with pain. "You must truly slay me; nor will I turn away my face from yours. May it come between you and your rest! Treacherous coward! Was it I that you saw in the blood-red pool?"

"Nay, thou moonstruck pup!" Pryce roared,

and angrily he raised the great sword for the final
blow. But as Hau Ferddas whistled over his head,
a shining hand reached from the rocks above and
grasped his wrist with steely force. Dacaerin cried
out in surprise and pain as the golden sword was
wrested from him.

The High King Eburacon stood on the moun-
taintop. Bevan loomed godlike against a thunder-
dark sky. Rage filled him like silver lightning;
Dacaerin stumbled back from the sight of him.
Bevan lifted his candent hand that held the sword
of Lyrdion; then with startling force he flung it
far down the mountainside. He leaped down between Cuin and Dacaerin, landing like a cat,
squarely on the ledge.

"Pryce of the Strongholds," he said in soft and
deadly tones, "I would not sully that fair blade of
the Beginnings with your blood. I will fight you
with steel and the skill my comrade has taught
me. What, man, say not that you have neglected
to bring your own unstolen sword!"

In wordless agitation Pryce produced a blade.
"Have at you, then!" Bevan exclaimed and moved
swiftly to the fray. Cuin bit his lip and trembled
as he watched, for Dacaerin was a seasoned fighter
who knew every trick of combat, and Bevan had
ever scorned the war-like trade. . . . But this day
Bevan fought with his own feral grace and with
the force of his wrath. Pryce Dacaerin was shaken
by the sudden turning of his fate, unnerved by
his failure. He staggered back before Bevan's
attack, then desperately turned to run for the
defile. But his haste betrayed him; stones slid
beneath his feet and he hurtled over the cliff. His
cry hung on the air for the long moment of his

falling. Bevan froze where he stood, staring after him.

"There are dragons in the Deep," he breathed, "and now there is another one." He leaned against the rock with lidded eyes and a face like death. Alarmed even in his vast relief, Cuin struggled toward him.

"Bevan! Are you hurt?"

"Nay," Bevan murmured. "The sea, Cuin; it pierces me."

"Duv, I forgot!" Cuin exclaimed. "Come away, Bevan, quickly!"

Bevan opened his eyes slowly. "Oh, Cuin, you bleed," he whispered, and tears wet his cheeks. Cuin stared, for he had never known his comrade to weep. Bevan turned his face to the stone and sobbed. With aching effort, Cuin put an arm around him.

"Come away," he urged gently.

Slowly, with arms on each other's shoulders, they made their way up to the defile and stumbled down the steep rocks beyond. Pain racked Cuin. He sat to catch his breath. Far below, he could see the ungainly lump that was his roan, lying still with Dacaerin's spear in its side. Pryce's tall red bay was nowhere to be seen.

"Where is your horse?" he asked Bevan when he could speak.

"I killed it with galloping hither." Sharp sorrow was in Bevan's voice. "Flessa lies dead below; it is just the two of us now, Cuin."

But Cuin was beyond speaking of Flessa. "By blood," he muttered, "I am as spent as a pauper's purse. I cannot go much farther."

"Just to the grass; then we shall rest."

But Cuin did not make it to the pasturelands.

The rocks came up to meet him, and he lay on them uncaring. Vaguely he perceived a file of horsemen along the distant Forest, and he heard Bevan hail them. Then he shut his eyes and forgot to notice more.

CHAPTER SIX

Cuin awoke to find himself lying on a soft bed in a vaulted chamber of stone. An old woman was watching him. She scurried away when she saw his opened eyes, and soon a stocky man stumped into the room, followed by a servant with a tray. Cuin recognized his host as the stalwart Owen of Twyth.

"So!" the chieftain exclaimed. "Your storm of sorrow came soon, hah?"

"Fast and fell." Cuin sat up gingerly to take the proffered drink. "How did I come here?"

"By mine eyes, 'tis not every day that we hear sword-play on the peaks, Cuin King's Man. I sent a patrol out to look, and they came back with you and your friend. That is a strange one, he! The big man leaned forward in innocent wonder. "No sooner had he seen you cared for than he must ride out again, no less, and came back with a great bundle under his arm. And a dead falcon, which he must needs lay to rest like a proper soul! Then he slept not the whole night, but paced and prowled about, with nary a light to guide him. He stopped here before dawn to see you, and the old woman swears his hand burned her arm. . . . Now he's off again, and all this time I've scarcely had three words from him. Who or what might he be?"

"Bevan of Eburacon, High King," Cuin replied quietly, "and he has stranger powers than the ones you have named. Where has he gone?"

"Southward, toward the sea. So that is the new-crowned King of Isle! And he came to you himself! You must be dear to him indeed. But who gave you your wounds?" Owen broke off, puzzled, for Cuin was not listening; he was pulling on his clothes.

"You've not yet eaten, lord!" Owen protested.

"I must go to him," Cuin said worriedly. "Pray point me the way."

Shaking his head and expostulating, Owen complied. To the south and east the land was steep but not lofty, lowering by degrees toward the estuary of the Gleaming River. Cuin picked his way along the ridge and down a sloping path beyond, to where Bevan sat overlooking the sea. The noise of the breakers was loud beneath him. He started as Cuin slid down to sit at his side.

"Cuin!" he exclaimed. "You should not be here!"

"Neither should you," Cuin retorted.

"You know what I mean," Bevan grumbled. "How do you feel?"

"Stiff, but no worse." Cuin settled himself painfully on the comfortless ledge and pulled a packet from his shirt. "Owen would not let me come off without food. Will you eat?"

"Nay, you eat." Bevan did not even glance at the meal; his eyes were on the sea.

"I thought it hurt you," Cuin remarked presently with his mouth full.

"As love hurts." Bevan turned to Cuin with aching eyes. "Though I never knew the veriest pang of it till lately. . . . Strange, Cuin, how fervently we fought those unmade men of the mantled lord! For I also was an unhearted thing, unknown to myself, until Celonwy my mother freed me from the spell of the white hart."

"Tell me," Cuin said.

They talked for hours, quietly retracing the interwoven threads of their lives, seeking the turnings that had led them to this place where, both sensed, destiny tottered on the wheel. "If only I had kept Hau Ferddas from mine uncle's hand," Cuin mourned.

"Small matter. His bid for power would have come soon or late," Bevan replied. "He was what he has been these many years. . . . I was a fool to trust him out of my sight."

"And I a fool and a coward to leave you with him, as he knew well I would," Cuin sighed. "Sword and maid have been our making and unmaking, it seems; both are bright blades of double edge . . . Where is Hau Ferddas, Bevan?"

"Well hid." Bevan gazed intently at the sea. Cuin gasped and clutched his hand; there were creatures in the deep. A fey green stare matched theirs from the breakers. Wideset wild and fearless eyes looked from under a tumult of wavewashed hair. Others blinked beyond. Cuin struggled to find his feet.

"Come away!" he shouted. "They are sylkies; they will drive you mad!" But Bevan had leaped to his feet, calling to them in his strange melodious tongue, pulling against Cuin's grip. The seafolk vanished swan-like beneath the waves. Bevan looked after them with yearning eyes, and Cuin grasped his trembling shoulders.

"Come away!" he charged him. "There are evil things in the sea; they will cozen you as power cozened Dacaerin."

"Evil!" Bevan turned on him like a startled deer. "Say not so, Cuin; they are my brothers, I who have none!" His eyes went awash like the sea, and then he hung his head and wept. Cuin put his arms around him, pierced with pity. The sun sank toward the endless water, and still they stood.

"Ever you were a stranger among us," Cuin whispered huskily at last.

"Two have loved me," Bevan replied dully, "two who most deserve the best of love. But I have never truly loved until now, Cuin, and now I love the sea."

The sun touched the waves with its golden disc. "Come away," Cuin said gently. "I cannot spend the night on this ledge, but I'll not leave without you, Bevan."

Silently they made their way back to Owen's stronghold. He welcomed them and set a feast before them, but Bevan scarcely touched the food. Cuin took early to his bed and slept heavily from the exhaustion of his wounds. Yet even in his slumber fear clutched his heart. When he awoke Bevan was nowhere to be found. Cuin knew where to look for him. He begged the favor of horses and provisions from Owen.

" 'Tis little I've seen of your King, my lord," the chieftain complained.

"He is not well in heart," Cuin confessed. "I must get him back to his bride. . . ." Owen was chuckling in his beard as Cuin left to search the sea-cliffs. "Come on," he said simply when he found Bevan. "It is time we were going."

Bevan came without a word, found his bundle and mounted his horse. Hau Ferddas hung heavy as a lance beneath his arm. He and Cuin rode silently through the day and camped in a forested valley that night. But in the morning when Cuin arose, Bevan was gone: horse, sword and all. His trail led plainly to the south and east. Cuin followed it with angry haste. At dusk he found Bevan sitting on the shingle at the bay of the Gleaming River. Salt waves lapped at his feet.

"I will not move from this place," Bevan said without warmth.

"What would you do, then!" Cuin shouted furiously. "Sit there until you starve? Or leap in, perchance? You have no gills, Bevan!"

"Nay," Bevan answered softly. "It is not the water alone that calls me, Cuin. There is something else. Its name is Elwestrand."

The word went through Cuin and left him weak. "Ellid deserves knowledge of this," he muttered.

"Go for her," Bevan ordered.

"How can I!" Cuin cried. "I dare not leave you, besotted as you are! You'll starve or drown before I can return!"

Bevan glanced at him sharply. "I am not entirely without honor," he told Cuin stiffly. "I will be here when you return; I give you my word."

Cuin regarded him doubtfully. "What can you swear by," he mused, "that I shall believe you?"

Bevan stalked to his bundle and tore Hau Ferddas from its wrappings. Savagely he thrust it into the shore at the mark of high tide. "By this," he snapped. "The fair sword of double edge. May it slay me if I fail you!"

"Well," Cuin stated, and rode away without another word. He would not sleep by the booming of the sea, a sound of endless dread to him. He rode inland until full dark had fallen and silence surrounded him. Then he stopped and sat by a fire; but there was no comfort for him in firelight that night.

More than a fortnight after Bevan had gone, Ellid still lingered on the Downs with Eitha and Celonwy. A few of Dacaerin's retainers stayed to bring them meat, but all others had left. Kael had long since regretfully departed to his people in the far north, in company with the tribesmen of Romany. The Firthola had gone to their ships and the lords to their holdings. Young Dene had led away the remaining men of Wallyn. The birds sang through the days, but Ellid could not enjoy them. She had never felt so alone.

Thus, on the day that Cuin cantered up from the west, she ran to greet him and kissed him joyfully, though she knew from his face that his news was bad. "What tidings?" she demanded as she released him.

He spoke not to her but to her mother, who stood at her side. "My aunt, your husband is dead. I am sorry."

"You have slain a dragon, you mean," Eitha replied harshly. "That is no cause for sorrow."

"Nay, I slew him not. He had Hau Ferddas, and I could not stand against him." Cuin still faced his aunt. "Bevan overpowered him."

"Then Bevan lives!" Ellid exclaimed thankfully.

"Ay, but he is not well." Cuin would not meet her eyes.

"Wounded? How?" She was frightened, not so much by his words as by his manner, for she had never known Cuin to speak to the ground.

"Nay, not wounded," Cuin mumbled. "He is not well in heart."

Ellid stared helplessly, and Celonwy grasped Cuin's arm. "Now tell me plainly what has chanced."

Cuin met the deepset eyes of this woman he had never seen before, and he knew at once that she would understand. "He sits by the sea."

"Then we must go to him with all haste," said Celonwy.

"Even so."

They left with the morning's dawn. Frail as she looked, Celonwy would have nothing to do with the stuffy horse-litter. She mounted a steed lightly aside, letting her pearly skirts flow over her feet. Gladly Ellid did the same, ignoring the stares of the onlookers. Eitha said nothing, but waved a brave farewell. She was not coming; she would travel with retainers to her husband's estate. Only Cuin would go with the others to the bay where Bevan waited.

Cuin led his party off with doubtful sighs. But he soon discovered that the women were good travelers. They forded the Gleaming River the first day and made the bay a week later. The sword still stood in its place on the beach, and Bevan waited beside it, gazing out to sea.

"Bevan!" Ellid hailed him. All the harmony of youthful longing was in her voice.

"Ellid," Bevan murmured as she sank down

beside him. "How I have wronged you." But he scarcely turned to look at her; his eyes were on the waves.

"Bevan," she asked him gently, "what is it that you see to delight you in that landless waste? It is a sight only of dread to me."

"Waste?" Bevan smiled faintly, still gazing. "Look again, my lady." As he spoke, bubbles brightened the quiet waters of the bay and a sleek silver head broke the surface. Ellid gasped and jumped back from the shore; Cuin stiffened and stood his ground. But Bevan and Celonwy watched the sea-drake with smiling ease. Another joined the first; they stared at their leisure and then dove, putting up a rainbow spray fairer than the fountains of Eburacon.

"The sea is a shining thing, yet vast and deep as the night," said Bevan in a low voice. "Worlds of marvel are hid on its reaches. The sea itself would be wonder enough, but I look also to what is beyond. To a sunset land called Elwestrand, a name I do not understand."

Cuin cursed in pain and turned away. But Celonwy came and knelt by Bevan's side. "My son," she told him softly, "how well I know the call you feel. At the time of the Accord, when my people agreed to give the sunlit lands over to the race of man, many set sail upon the Deep, even as others took to the deeps of earth. It was the sea that first brought us to Isle. Ancient and mighty is the love of it in our blood.

"Yet consider well, my son. Your father's blood first laid its hold on you, and you have cast in your lot with his people. His realm has bitter need of you; too long have its folk lived in bloody fear. Now men have found hope in you, and in your

name they have lived a season of peace. Pel
Blagden is laid low, but forget not that the Stone
has spoken of worse to come. It has charged you
above all to serve your father's folk and to
strengthen them against the evil that will come
from the east: for one who is called a King is one
who is called to serve for all his life."

"Though I could not give my heart to my people," Bevan answered heavily, "yet I would have
given them the gifts of life and youth. I struggled
to my depths for Coradel Orre, but it shattered
with the strain of wills. That sundering ripped
me like a leaf, but it was a twinge compared to the
tug that is on me now. If I tear myself from the
sea I will be a useless sundered thing, a half-
King. The best part of me will die to haunt this
place, even before I die entirely."

"Folly take him who follows the seal!" Cuin
exclaimed.

"And folly follow him who does not know his
own heart." Bevan met Cuin's gaze with rueful
eyes. "I have done such folly aplenty this year
past, but today my way is clear to me. I can be
no King, nor longer cast my lot in Isle. The sea
summons me. I will lay my life upon her tides."

His words hung on the air like a doom.
They all stood stricken with its falling. In her
valley far to the north, Ylim sighed and started a
new thread to her web, a blood-red skein. And in
the treasure room at Caer Eitha, the Speaking
Stone cracked in two. Ever after, water ran down
from the break like mute tears.

Bevan built himself a boat. With his argent
hands he fashioned it out of the fairest woods of

the Welandais Forest, and every gift of his power
was in it. During the long month of its making
his mother Celonwy lay serenely dying. She was
sheltered by a hut Cuin had hastily built of sap-
lings and bark. Ellid attended her, and Cuin
brought them meat. Bevan seemed scarcely to eat
or have need of food, still less of talk or companionship. He moved and breathed only for his
ship and the sea.

Those were dark days for Cuin and Ellid. They
had tried every means of plea and persuasion on
Bevan to no avail. Cuin's will was stubborn and
set to angry conflict. But Ellid realized early that
her husband's veriest heart had never been hers;
she acceded to his departure with a proud grace
that served to mask her floundering despair. All
the structure that she had built for her life seemed
to have come tumbling around her, and she moved
in a directionless void. She clung to her daily tasks
for comfort, and lavished her thwarted tenderness
upon the frail woman in her care.

"There is no need for you to fret so, dear,"
Celonwy told her placidly one day. "Death is no
great matter, though Bevan seems to think it is.
People die every day."

Ellid shrank from her words. "Folk die com-
monly, indeed," she mumbled, "and that is fright-
ful enough! But what must be our fright when a
goddess passes?"

Celonwy regarded her in gentle amusement. "Do
you think the moon will darken when I go?" she
smiled. "But it was there long before I lived, and
long after I am gone it will remain."

Ellid stared, trying to comprehend. "It is the

moon that gives me light," Celonwy went on cheerfully, "not the contrary. . . . I have been a moon goddess because I took the moon as my mentor. It has taught me wisdom enough to know that I am not very different from you, Ellid Ciasifhon. Had you been one of our fellowship, you would have been a deity of flight."

"You mock me," Ellid whispered, dazed.

"Nay, no whit! What is a god or a goddess but a person who dreams? We children of Duv are those who have lived long and remembered magics and mysteries out of the Beginnings. It was that which set us apart, but that is ended now that Coradel Orre is gone. I depart but a little before my fellows."

"Does Bevan know?" Ellid asked in shock.

"Nay, he does not. Keep it from him, dear. I fear he could not understand how rightly he has done. Coradel Orre became a horror in the hands of a god, and it could hardly have done better in the hands of men. . . . It is well that it was destroyed, and it is meet that the children of the Great Mother should make an end. Our time is done, and another order of beings prepares to take our place."

Ellid could not understand half of what she had heard, but there was reassurance in Celonwy's friendly fortitude. She and the failing goddess talked often, and gradually Ellid came to better comprehend Bevan the son of the immortals: his long-standing quarrel with death, the overwhelming strength of the summons that drew him, and most of all his awful and abiding loneliness, he who was neither god nor man. "I scarcely touched the surface of his pain," Ellid murmured.

"Nor shall any, until he lets them, dear. He has not yet learned the wisdom of surrender to the tides of his life."

Cuin did not have the comfort of such talk. He moved through the days in hurt and solitary wrath. He would not lift a hand to help Bevan's labor, but lost no chance to sit by and speak his mind. Bevan responded with unfailing and indifferent courtesy, which galled Cuin to helpless fury.

"Messengers bring word of your kingdom," he told Bevan bitterly one day. "There is rumor of war in the heartland. The stewards of the strongholds plot to move against the young lord of Wallyn. Eitha cannot control them."

"I am sorry," Bevan replied, as if to news of a distant place.

"You should be," Cuin retorted icily.

Bevan faced him stoically. "Cuin, nothing binds you to me. Go set things to rights."

The calm words struck Cuin like a knife. "I have never failed to follow you," he whispered tightly.

"You cannot follow me where I go now." Bevan ran his hand over the smooth flanks of his ship.

The truth seared Cuin like flame; he cried out with the pain of it. Bevan strode to him quickly and held him.

"So you know at last that I must go," he breathed. All indifference was gone from his voice.

"Ay." Tears choked Cuin, and he could not say more.

"Then pray quarrel with me no longer, Cuin," Bevan requested gently, "for I would part from you in all love. . . . Must you go to Wallyn?"

"Nay." Cuin raised aching eyes. "The season moves on apace. Cold will put a halt to all such schemes of men. . . . Bevan, I bow to your will, but still I do not understand. How can things have come so to naught for us?"

"Fate turns quaintly." Bevan sat and quirked his grave face into a smile. "Yet there is this to think on: an end will ever be a beginning. You will be King, Cuin; mark it."

"What?" Cuin whispered.

"The heir of the throne of Lyrdion will wed the Queen of Eburacon, she who is fairer than the sunlight on the Downs. . . . You will be doubly King, Cuin. You will have Hau Ferddas to enforce your will, though I think you might scarcely need it, for you are much man. May you yet bring peace to this blood-crazed land."

"You burden me more than I can bear," Cuin groaned. "Hau Ferddas! I would rather hurl it into the sea!"

"As you will." Bevan arched delicate eyebrows. "But surely you will better care for that other bright blade, she whom the bards name Ellid Lightwing."

"Mothers help me," Cuin muttered, and wandered dazedly into the Forest. Singing softly, Bevan went back to his boat. Through the shortening days of autumn he wrought and sang:

> A speaking stone, a shining brand
> Summoned the lords of all the land.
> But what is this call that summons me
> Across the ever-sundering sea?
> What is this call of Elwestrand,
> A name I do not understand?

Fate is a lovely woman, and
Fair are her gifts to mortal man.
A winsome Queen, a silver crown,
A turn of the wheel; all tumbles down.
Where is the friend who can come with me
Across the ever-sundering sea?

A sorrowing stone, a seeress' hand
Grieve for my flight to seek the strand.
For Death is a mighty doomster; still
I may yet stand to foil his will.
Is this the power of Elwestrand,
The place beyond the sun's command?

Two days before the full moon, on a night
when golden leaves fell from the trees like snow
in the pale light, Celonwy died without a sound.
Cuin and Bevan buried her where great fir trees
shaded the silver river as it widened to a silver
bay. Ellid shivered in the brooding shadows.

"It is a dreaming place," Bevan explained to
her, "a place of the fair dark even in daylight, but
never without a whisper of shine. It suits her. Let
us go."

The next morning, on a day that frost had
turned to crystal, Bevan slid his ship into the
gleaming waters of the bay. Like a new-birthed
steed the craft shuddered, and like a fledgling swan
it skimmed away. Of itself it swam, ever more
graceful and dartingly swift. Ellid and Cuin stood
agape with the wonder of its motion.

"It lives!" Ellid gasped.

"It is quick with all the surging life of the trees,"
Bevan said. "I but set it free."

Cuin's heart ached. "Oh, Bevan, how you could have freed this Isle," he grieved.

"Think of it no more, Cuin. What is gone is gone." Bevan turned and called a melodious command. The boat floated like a leaf to the shore by his feet, and Bevan set a plank to its side.

"Would you go into the teeth of the winter!" Cuin exclaimed. "And what of provision?"

"I will not feel cold or hunger. I will but gaze and dream. Fear not for me."

"I am your wedded wife," Ellid whispered. "I should sail by your side." But her face was sick with fear at the thought of it.

"Nay, Ellid!" Bevan earnestly took her hand. "You are wed to me only by empty words of men. Heed them not, but heed your heart. You are a creature of sunlight and firelight and all warm comfort; you have no abode in the dreaming twilit lands beyond the setting sun." His face was more than grave; it was sad with a sadness she had never seen in him. "Truly Ellid, I love you well even now, but in wisdom I never should have wooed you! We are different as day and night, you and I."

"And I also am one who would live in the light," Cuin muttered.

"Ay. You are much alike, you two, and alike in your loves. I know you have never ceased to cherish her happiness, Cuin, and I know she loves you well, though she does not know it herself. . . ." Bevan placed Ellid's slender hand into Cuin's weathered palm and clasped his own fair hands over theirs. "She is not a thing to be given or taken, Cuin; court her for her consent, I charge you. May the Mothers bless you both and give you sons."

Ellid laughed bitterly. "Mothers in a world of men! Reverence of women is gone, Bevan, and you might as well make a gift of me! Already strange shaven priests have come from the east to summon our people to their rites. They call their god Father, and speak of his tormented son."

"I hope a time may yet come," Bevan murmured, "when all folk may speak only of the One who is father and mother of us all." He embraced Cuin and Ellid hastily, then turned to his waiting ship. Cuin stopped him.

"Your crown," he said, and proffered the rayed silver diadem of Eburacon.

Bevan eyed him quizzically. "I'll be no King where I go! Have I not said that you should have need of it?"

"If I am truly to be a King, I can find a crown." Cuin faced him steadily. "But I'll not use yours, Bevan. Take it."

Bevan smiled faintly at the stubborn glint in Cuin's eyes. "I will take the crown if you will keep the sword. Pact?"

"Pact," Cuin acceded, and they touched hands. Bevan took the crown on his arm and once more turned to depart, but suddenly Cuin could not bear the silence. He seized Bevan and embraced him hard. "Forget not that you are loved here," he whispered fiercely.

"I will not forget," Bevan replied softly, "but I will not return, Cuin; think not so. Farewell, good friend. Farewell, Ellid." Quickly he strode onto his ship and threw away the plank. Cuin went to stand by Ellid's side.

"Go with all blessing!" she called.

The ship started like a stag and leaped away from the shore. Cuin and Ellid waved, but Bevan stood like a shining figurehead in the bow. His hair parted like raven's wings in the breeze of his passing; his dark eyes were rapt. Far out in the bay the silver sea-drakes arched their glistening necks above the water in salute. The swift boat skimmed between them, then swirled away until it was but a shape of grace on the water, soon lost in the sparkle of the sea.

Cuin and Ellid blinked and faced each other with stunned eyes. "How could he leave you without a tear?" Cuin murmured.

"By the Mothers, I scarcely knew him," Ellid replied heavily. "Nor has he known me, though I would have cleaved to him till death. Come, let us go. I cannot be soon enough gone from this place."

They walked wearily to the horses. "I dare say you will want me on a pillion now," Ellid muttered.

Cuin took her by her waist and set her on her steed for answer. "Let you ride like a Queen of the Mothers," he told her, "now and always. Hold your head high, Ellid." He went and tugged the golden sword from its place on the shore, wrapping it in his cloak. Then he stopped and stared at Ellid. Her head was bent, and great silent tears were slipping down her face. He went to her and held her hand, looking up at her in unspoken query.

"Cuin," she sorrowed. "Dear Cuin. All powers forbid that I should hurt you ever again! But I am of as many minds as there are sparrows in the trees, and my heart is stone within me."

"There will be time," Cuin told her gently. "Time for your healing, and time for me to woo you as you deserve, I who once thought you no more than my right. . . . But do not think of me this day. I will attend you to your mother's home, no more. Are you ready?"

She nodded, and they turned their horses to the north. By his side she rode through the dying days, and he reached out to her only with his glance.

EPILOGUE

A year later, when leaves once again hung
golden on the trees, Cuin rode with Ellid to a little
valley he had entered once before. On his head
Cuin wore a golden crown. It had been a strange
and bloody summer, and Ellid had held her head
high against fearful strain; there had been talk of
burning her as a witch who had destroyed her
husband. Cuin had risen to power largely to protect her. At first he had sought only that the
renegade stewards of Dacaerin should submit to
the authority Eitha had given him. But battle led
to battle, and then friends who remembered him
from Blagden had upheld him and named him
their High King. Even Kael had been drawn in.
The outlaw chieftains were mostly quieted now;
the realm was held in uneasy truce and winter
would enforce it. But Cuin dreaded the coming of
spring, and he craved the counsel of the seeress.

Ancient Ylim looked not a day changed from
his last sight of her. She still sat before her loom.
"Welcome, Cuin Kellarth! Welcome, Ellid Ciasifhon," she greeted them. Her smile was all in her
eyes.

"Sweet is the sound of those names in my ear, Ylim," Cuin replied.

"Why so, Cuin?" Ellid asked. She looked around with wide and wondering eyes at the placid old woman and the cottage and commonplace scene that all glowed like new-created things.

"It is the elder tongue, such as Bevan spoke," Cuin told her. "It gladdens me even to hear it, though I know it not."

"Steadfast man and lightwing maiden," Ylim beckoned, "come and look on my web, for that is why you are here, is it not?"

The stag was gone, lost behind a curtain of bloody red. But then the hue softened to that of firelight and richest sunlight and red-gold like the mighty sword of Lyrdion. Indeed, the sword was there, and past it flashed a bright form of winged beauty. "Flessa!" Ellid cried.

"Men still call me Falconer King," Cuin marveled, "though the bird is gone from me."

"Nay, she cleaves to you yet." Ylim regarded them with her all-knowing gaze. "Ellid Ciasifhon was always your comfort, even when she knew it not."

"Something of me is in all such flying things," Ellid murmured, "and of them in me."

"Even so."

"Still, it was not your hope and vision, Ylim," Cuin said slowly, "that we should be together."

"Not while Bevan of the Argent Hand yet walked the sunlit lands," the seeress replied promptly. "I grieve that he is gone; great is the evil that he could have thwarted, he and his heirs. But the One is not like a twig or a leaf that can be turned aside from its purpose. Out of tragedy yet that power will shape good."

Ellid sank down by Ylim's knee. "Grandmother, I do not understand," she whispered. "What is the evil from the east?"

The old woman's eyes grew cloudy. "A veriest blight and bane," she mourned, "spreading and shadowing even from the Source, evil as much greater than evil of Pel as the wolf is greater than the rat. . . . But let it not frighten you, little daughter." She placed a dry, wrinkled hand on Ellid's head. "It will not be for many lives of men."

"Yet already the One sought to prepare us?" Cuin exclaimed.

"Ay. Men would have rallied around Bevan and his heirs. . . . Surely it is no fault of yours, Cuin, that you bear human scars and raise hands of merely human power! You and yours will reign long and bring peace to Isle, make a green and sunny land of it. But in the end peace will fail; not even Hau Ferddas will save it."

"That is a saying of no hope," Cuin muttered.

Ylim almost laughed; her ageless face creased into a smile. "I have looked far to find you doom! But now it seems I must look yet farther to find you hope! Forget not that the One labors ever for our weal. In those distant days, the heirs of Bevan shall return from Elwestrand. The first of them shall be Veran, but the greatest of them shall be Hal. And his comrade on these shores shall be a scion of your line."

"Then Bevan lives?" Ellid exclaimed.

"Of course he lives."

"And still it is meet," Cuin asked softly, "that I should be King?"

"Did not the Very King tell you so? Ay, it is meet. Yet look not to bloodstained Lyrdion or shadowed Eburacon, but build your court afresh at the place of laverocs, a spot of fair omen. And doubt not that it is meet for you to wed the Very Queen, she whom you have loved for these many years. There is some harm in it, for she is your kin; such was the custom of shameful Lyrdion. But you are both of good heart, and Isle shall rejoice in your sons."

Ellid and Cuin glanced at each other with glowing eyes from which all trace of uncertainty had gone. Cuin reached for her hand.

"We have no need of hollow rites," he said.

"Come to my bed this night," Ellid answered him softly.

They turned and wandered wordlessly from the cottage; already Ylim had gone back to her loom. It was a two-days' ride to Caer Eitha, but they would make it last for three. Well might bode the begetting of a King amidst the regal gold and russet leaves.

Fantasy Novels
from
POCKET BOOKS

___83217   THE BOOK OF THE DUN COW
Walter Wangerin, Jr. $2.50
*"Far and away the most literate and intelligent
story of the year."—The New York Times*

___43131   THE WHITE HART
Nancy Springer $2.50
*"It has everything; a believable fantasy world...
a lovely, poignant book."*
—Marion Zimmer Bradley

___82912   BEAUTY Robin McKinley $1.95
*"The most delightful first novel I've read in
years...I was moved and enchanted."—Peter S.
Beagle, author of THE LAST UNICORN*

___83281   CHARMED LIFE $2.25
"An outstanding success."—Andre Norton

___83294   ARIOSTO
Chelsea Quinn Yarbo $2.25
*"Colorful and exciting...a vivid tapestry come
to life...superb!"—Andre Norton*

___82958   THE ORPHAN
Robert Stallman $2.25
*"An exciting blend of love and violence, of
sensitivity and savagery."—Fritz Leiber*

POCKET BOOKS Department FAN
1230 Avenue of the Americas, New York, N.Y. 10020

Please send me the books I have checked above. I am enclosing $_____
(please add 50¢ to cover postage and handling for each order, N.Y.S. and N.Y.C.
residents please add appropriate sales tax). Send check or money order—no
cash or C.O.D.s please. Allow up to six weeks for delivery.

NAME_____

ADDRESS_____

CITY_____STATE/ZIP_____

77